MURGATREUD'S EMPIRE

Bamber Gascoigne, thirty-eight, has been chairman of the highly successful British television series 'University Challenge' since 1962. He was drama critic of the *Spectator* from 1961 to 1963 and of the *Observer* from 1963 to 1964. His other books are *Twentieth Century Drama*, *World Theatre: An Illustrated History*, and *The Great Moghuls*, a study of the emperors of India which is illustrated with photographs by his wife Christina. This is his first novel.

MURGATREUD'S EMPIRE

BAMBER GASCOIGNE

QUARTET BOOKS   LONDON

Published by Quartet Books Limited 1973
27 Goodge Street, London W1P 1FD

First published in Great Britain by Jonathan Cape Ltd 1972
Reprinted 1972

Copyright © 1972 by Bamber Gascoigne

ISBN 0 704 31063 5

Printed in Great Britain by
Hunt Barnard Printing Ltd, Aylesbury, Bucks.

MURGATREUD'S EMPIRE

I

A shrill yodelling cry in the tropical undergrowth. Murgatreud, born Murgatroyd but changed the spelling for business reasons in the modern world, just as his grandfather, born Murgatreud, had changed the spelling for business reasons fifty years before, opened one painful eye and wondered where in gottes himmel he was.

And well he might. Only a few yards away, beyond some large moist leaves, crouched an incredibly small black man. His breath pounded in and out through his mouth like a dog's. The ominous yodel rang out again, nearer now. The tiny Negro edged further back. He became blurred, to Murgatreud's fevered eye, seeming to expand and shrink like an image groping for focus. And Murgatreud slipped back into darkness.

When he surfaced again, the little man was even nearer, and Murgatreud could see now what terrified him. Another man, equally black and only very slightly larger, was moving through the dark tangle of creepers and rotting branches. He held before him a bow, longer than himself, and in it a half-drawn arrow. Hardly the best weapon for this web of vegetation, it kept getting entangled and deflected, but most of the time it pointed clearly enough towards his prey – and beyond him at Murgatreud.

Murgatreud had been vaguely aware of a metallic object against his arm. Slowly, with excruciating effort, he lifted it and let it drop against the hunched back of the fugitive. The little head spun round. The eyes dilated in the first moment of shock, then narrowed down on to the weapon that Murgatreud offered. And as his pursuer turned half away for another yodel, the little man leapt from among the leaves, swinging in a high arc the strip of metal, two feet long, six inches wide, jagged at both ends but with a knife-edge along the straight side.

The yodeller struck his high note as the blow fell. The blade sliced into the skull to a depth of two or three inches, where it stuck, but in Murgatreud's mind the image continued until the body was split down the middle as far as a last retaining ligament at the scrotum, clothes and armour and internal organs all neatly divided, as in a medieval manuscript which he had recently bought in Zagreb, sold in Los Angeles. The victim seemed to stand for a moment as if in surprise, with the blade in his head. Then he fell forward. Murgatreud's ally turned back to where he lay. And the fat white entre-preneur's final image, before he again faded into unconscious-ness, was of the little black face coming slowly down nearer to his, tentatively, much as a child might inspect a dying cow.

When Murgatreud came round for the third time, he had the distinct impression he was naked. There was still a small black man peering down at him, but the details had changed. In place of the green vegetation, a halo of sky framed and blurred the face. A white line sliced across it, flickering like fitful neon. Two bright jagged dugs drooped on either side, as if being milked into Murgatreud's pulsing eyes.

In a final grab at survival he forced himself, against the clatter and thump in his skull, to focus on the shifting details before him. For one moment he held them still, and saw a young savage in typical finery. A strip of smooth white bone pierced his nose, jutting out as proud as a well-waxed moustache. Heavy shells had extended grotesquely the lobes of his ears. But he looked anxious rather than hostile, and in that brief moment he opened his mouth.

'Seems in a frightfully dicky state,' he said, 'but I get the impression he may pull through.'

He spoke in the rapid but rarefied tones of the B.B.C. between the wars. Murgatreud gave up. His eyes relinquished their hold on the savage's features and he abandoned himself, almost with a sense of relief, to the encroaching chaos.

He was aware of only one bitter regret. In spite of foreseeing so many times this very contingency, no one had been given the number of the bank account in Geneva. Now the little children would get nothing. The waifs, the spastics, the undernourished, the skinny ones and the fat ones, the unloved, the brave and incomplete Thalidomides, all of them, nothing. This was too bitter an end. And for the third time, like a drowning man, he went under.

II

Nothing like this had ever happened in the clearing before. A member of the tribe had come panting up the hill, brandishing a bright strip of metal clotted at one end with blood and hair. This was wonder enough, but he had then announced that there was a magic monster lying blue and vast in the forest below. A party set off to round it up, armed with long bows and arrows and with tasselled spears. And someone was sent to tell the white men at the far end of the village the remarkable news.

By the time the hunters arrived back there was an impressive reception committee in the clearing. On one side of an improvised trestle table, set up under the shade of a tree, stood the chief of the tribe in full regalia. The shells clinging to his face and neck would have filled a modest showcase. On his head waved a magnificent spray of cassowary plumes, the total produce of many months of a group of these unfortunate birds which were pampered with every care and tenderness in wicker cages, except for the two days in the year when they were almost plucked alive to replenish the chief's headgear. Around him stood his four wives. Like their husband, they were naked except at the loins. Like him, they were lavishly decorated, but in more barbaric style. Their beauty marks were savagely raised weals, on back and belly and around the breasts. They had been given these precious scars in childhood, and they now spent much of their time improving in identical fashion their own daughters' chances in the world. With a sharpened shell they would make a long horizontal slice into the young girl's skin. And day after day, as a scab tried to form, it was teased and stirred with thorns until the flesh had risen high in protest and a permanent weal was assured. But the faces were spared, and with their delicate black features the chief's four wives were undoubtedly pretty. Indeed, they were, in every sense of the word, petite. The chief, whose name was Alalo, stood four foot six without his plumes. His wives averaged four inches less.

On the other side of the trestle table was an even odder assortment of people. There was another member of the tribe, a young man of about twenty, adorned like the chief with shells and with a long straight bone through his nose. He was known as J.K. There was a girl of the same age, who would perhaps have looked much like the chief's wives except that her body was unscarred and she wore a tattered skirt in a chequered table-cloth material and what appeared to be a very old crepe bandage bound tightly round her breasts. This was Teresa.

And there were two white men – or jaundiced brown men, after twenty years in this climate. One, tall and thin, might have measured some six foot four inches if straightened out, but he had subsided long ago into an S. There was no sign of a behind in his baggy trousers, which seemed to conceal only a hinge. Above it his spine arched one way, below it his legs arched the other. He was Dr Manning, one-time King's Scholar of Eton College and a graduate of a small medical school in west London. He carried an ancient Gladstone-bag.

The other European, much shorter and by comparison almost plump, had a shock of red hair and a look of boyish excitement which made it hard to believe he was in his mid-forties. He was wearing a cassock which ended in shreds above his ankles, and which had bleached almost to a dirty white, like abandoned black-out material. He held before him, with outstretched arm, an elaborate brass crucifix. This was Father O'Halloran, who years ago had drifted almost automatically from the College of the Sacred Heart on the banks of the Liffey to the Little Brothers of Mercy behind Kildare Place, but had come a long way since.

Like a grotesque cortège, twelve pygmies staggered up the rough slope into the clearing. On their shoulders they bore an unusually large fat white dead man, his head flopping from side to side as the bearers lurched on. What the reception committee saw coming towards them was a vast face upside down, scant hairs hanging vertical from a pink and plushy skull.

'Praise be to God,' murmured Father O'Halloran to Dr Manning, 'a proper Christian burial after twenty years.'

'How do you know he's a Christian?'

'Oh, God Almighty, don't say that. You don't think after so long the good Lord might have sent us ... ?'

As soon as the body was securely on the trestle table, O'Halloran inspected the face in an attempt to establish its creed. But features were not this corpse's strong point. Any racial characteristic which the bone structure might once have revealed had long ago been blurred in the indiscriminate march of flesh. All that was left was the pudgy fluid face of a man used to a lifetime of excess – something which any decent religion would surely welcome with open arms on its deathbed.

'Whatever he is,' said Father O'Halloran, 'I think we'll have him.' He made a cross on his own chest and then

5

repeated it on the chest of the corpse. But his fingers had to make a detour, a kink in the lateral bar, to find their way round the doctor's stethoscope. Wasting no time, Manning had removed it from the Gladstone-bag and applied it straight to the outside of the blue nylon flying-jacket.

'He's alive,' said the doctor.

'Oh well,' assented the priest, 'of course that's even better, then, definitely.'

A complete check was clearly necessary, and within moments the nimble fingers of Chief Alalo's four wives, coping dexterously with zips, buttons, nylon bows and even press-studs, had revealed the patient in his entirety. He was a remarkable sight, naked in the jungle clearing, a pink undulating mass against a background of dark green foliage. It was as though a bright inflatable dinghy had been abandoned in the Palm House at Kew.

The impression that the body had been blown up was accentuated by the leeches which had crept under his clothes. Black, firm projections, already nearly gorged, they had just the look of rubber valves. It seemed that if they were removed, the great body must sigh and crumple to an empty bag.

Dr Manning shifted the loathsome worms about the body, to greater medical effect. After twenty years in the jungle his Gladstone-bag contained, apart from his stethoscope, only a set of surgical tools smeared against rust with a heavy layer of Vaseline. His supplies had lasted less than two years. His last Western bandage had found its final resting-place as Teresa's bust-bodice, as the two British gentlemen had taught her to call it. And now Manning practised only the traditional medicine of old Europe and the jungle, in which leeches played an immoderately large part. The chief's wives were rubbing the body with various ointments while the doctor completed his inspection.

'Multiple contusions,' he finally announced, 'and of course concussion, otherwise a hundred per cent. A miracle.'

'A miracle indeed,' echoed Father O'Halloran, tilting the brass crucifix up at the sky. 'You're not really thinking he might be a Jew?'

6

'Ask him yourself, old boy, you should soon be able to.'

The priest started back up the hill to make his own hut ready to receive the patient. Dr Manning returned his instruments to the Gladstone-bag.

'You keep an eye on him, J.K.,' he said, 'while I give Father a hand with his accommodation.'

But Manning was only thirty yards away when J.K. almost shouted: 'I think ... I think he's ... yes, he is ... he's opening his eyes.'

The pygmies crowded round, but Manning remained where he was. He knew the patient would seem to surface several times before he came round entirely.

'How does he look?' he called down the slope. He enjoyed giving the boy this sort of responsibility.

J.K. peered into the pale face. Those puffy eyelids were being forced apart, but the little eyes in their pink cavities looked distraught, vacant, disorganized.

'Seems in a frightfully dicky state,' he reported. Then, realizing that something more positive was called for, something in the nature of a diagnosis from the man on the spot, he added, in an unconscious imitation of Dr Manning's own dry manner, 'but I get the impression he may pull through.'

III

And pull through of course he did. If Murgatreud had the appearance of rubber, he also shared much of its resilience. His multiple contusions turned blue, then black, then a mottled purple, and finally were no more than a faint cirrus effect in the skin. But within a week, when they were still in the black stage, he was pottering around the camp, poking his nose and often a fat finger into whatever was cooking, and responding to all the unfamiliar sights and customs with an incomprehensible expletive which sounded like 'hot ferdomma'.

Manning and O'Halloran each had a small hut at the top end of the village. For the first night O'Halloran had moved in with the doctor, but it was no more than a day's work to build a third hut. The entire pygmy tribe lent a hand. Nobody wanted to spend a moment longer than was necessary out of sight of the fascinating monster.

Strong bamboo canes were cut in the jungle and were worked a little way into the ground for the uprights of the small house. Others were fixed from a roof-beam down to the eaves to complete the open framework. The structure was much like an Elizabethan timber-frame cottage, except that the main supports were lashed together with vine, and the spaces between them would be filled with woven leaves rather than brick. With fresh palms available almost immediately overhead, Murgatreud's house was ready on the second day for him to move in – or rather be moved, one of the more laborious parts of the whole operation. Even his bed, again a bamboo frame with woven springs of leaf and fibre, was ready for the occasion. O'Halloran returned to his own hut. The white man's compound at the end of the village was already back to normal, but enlarged by fifty per cent or rather more.

Manning and O'Halloran were at least as interested as any of the pygmies in the new arrival, their only visitor in twenty years. The mystery of how he had dropped in was among the first to be solved. As he came round from his coma, in the anxiety-ridden state of concussion and shock, he began fretting about an elusive problem which was eventually deciphered as 'getting the bits'. 'Bits bitte,' he had suddenly flung at a startled Father O'Halloran, who at that time, thinking Murgatreud was still unconscious, was trying to lever him up to change the soiled grasses which served as bedpan or nappy to the patient. 'Bits bitte,' he had yelled, and at other times, 'Mayday,' or, 'Pezzi hot ferdomma,' or, in final exasperation, 'Oy, da schmuck, wotta dumbkopf.'

O'Halloran was baffled, but Manning deciphered the gist of all this. If foreign phrases were to be bandied about in this fashion, he too could compete.

'Simple enough,' he said, 'it's a *cri de coeur* from a wandering mind – always assuming that the mind can be said to have a heart and that heart a larynx – a simple *cri de coeur* asking for our help in putting together the pieces. The pieces of his life, the pieces of his memory, the pieces of his mind itself, O'Halloran.'

But Manning was wrong. All that Murgatreud was worried about was the pieces of his aeroplane. By the third day he was lucid, and Manning and O'Halloran were able to discover that he had been piloting himself from Manila to Queensland. Over the centre of New Guinea his engine behaved strangely and he lost height, but he had delayed too long before fitting his parachute. When he saw that he was about to plough into the tops of the jungle trees, he pressed the button of his ejector seat, and as the plane tipped a wing, spun, sliced through a tree and disintegrated, Murgatreud had traced a graceful arc through the air, hugging a fully furled parachute to his bosom. The tangled and yet supple mesh of the tropical forest had acted much as a series of nets for an acrobat. Murgatreud had bounced and bundled his way down through successive layers of vegetation, to land concussed and contused but miraculously unbroken on the soft dank mulch of millennia.

All round him in the jungle were fragments of his plane, and close to hand a jagged slice of the propeller. It was this that in a brief moment of consciousness he had handed to a member of the pygmy tribe among whom he was now living, who had used it to slice deep into the skull of a pygmy from another village.

Among the pieces of his aeroplane, Murgatreud was particularly impatient to recover two large black boxes. They contained, he said, his emergency kit, and were of crush-proof steel designed for just such a predicament as this. So the man with the slice of propeller – a proud possession

on which the matted blood and hair were carefully preserved –
led a search-party down to the scene of the crash. On the
first two evenings they returned with an extraordinary assortment of twisted scraps of metal from the fuselage of the plane,
but without the precious boxes. On the third day, one of the
two was found. It was inordinately heavy, and only after
hours of labour by a great many pygmies was it levered and
tumbled up the hill to Murgatreud's hut. It was a powerful
short-wave battery-operated transmitter-receiver, but it was
useless without its special accessories for operation outside
the plane – and these were in the other box, of which there
was still no sign. Murgatreud's impatience mounted, in step
with his improving health. On the seventh day it was at last
discovered in the thick undergrowth and was dragged up to
the camp.

The key was on Murgatreud's wrist, taped to the back
of one of his two watches. With the whole village standing
around for yet another revelation, he lifted the lid of the
chest, almost undented in the catastrophe. There was revealed
a dry, gleaming world of precision, a sight that made Manning's Gladstone-bag with its bundles of Vaselined scalpels
and tongs look like the sweepings of a workshop floor.
Neatly spread out in the lid, in tailored pockets of foam, was
a wide range of basic tools, from hammer and hack-saw and
chisel to monkey-wrench and adjustable spanner. But the eye
was drawn rapidly from this initial display to the more
mesmerizing shape of a squat black automatic lying on its
side in its own padded lair on the left of the chest. Beside it,
a leather belt made a pretty pattern, curled round on itself
and containing between each loop a series of little brass
circles. To the right of this arsenal came the medicine – neat
rows of unbreakable plastic containers, each with a different
label; plump bundles of bandages in polythene, squashed
tighter than the rush hour; three hypodermic syringes of
differing sizes; and dozens of boxes of pills. The remainder
of the chest was filled with larger pieces of equipment.
To the unscientific eyes of Manning and O'Halloran, there
seemed sufficient variety to repeat every observation or

experiment known to man. There were lenses mounted on calibrated scales, there were springs and balances in delicate conjunction, there were knobs and levers galore and a series of heavy manuals bound in washable black plastic. But Murgatreud, after a brief check that everything was in place and unbroken, was interested only in the radio section, a lift-out container holding an operator's head-phones, yards and yards of flex and the component parts of a very elaborate aerial. The cavity which remained when this was lifted out revealed a more intimate space at the bottom, occupied largely by scattered packets of chewing-gum and pages cut from *Playboy*. Murgatreud plugged in his ear-phones and spun the knobs on his receiver, and was soon rewarded by the gay uninhibited cackle of radio atmospherics. His lifeline to civilization was secure.

With his newly recovered equipment Murgatreud moved fast, or as fast as nature would allow. During the latter part of the following morning, still with a rapt audience of the two resident Europeans and a great many pygmies, he levelled his air sextant at the sun, using its built-in bubble of air to give him in this hilly country an artificial horizon. By taking a reading every few seconds he was able to establish almost exactly the moment at which the sun passed its zenith. This gave him local noon, and he set one of his two wrist-watches accordingly. He compared this with his other watch (it wound for a week, he informed the audience, and told the time in Liberia) and after some scribbled calculations in the ample palm of his hand he was able to announce a fact of which Manning and O'Halloran had lived twenty years in untroubled ignorance. They were precisely at longitude 142·4 East.

When darkness fell that evening, Murgatreud again pointed his sextant at the sky. And with the help of two of his black plastic volumes, the *Air Almanac* and *Sight Reduction Tables for Air Navigation*, he was able to complete the picture. They were also precisely at latitude 7·76 South. Meanwhile a pygmy had scrambled up a near-by tree, among the brilliant orchids which perched in the topmost branches, and had fixed there a directive antenna aimed at Monrovia, where President Tubman still held free court. It was connected by a long umbilical cord to Murgatreud below.

This tornado of scientific activity, as unfamiliar in these surroundings as if Einstein had been let loose in a monastery, reached its peak later that same night at 21.50 local time when Murgatreud, his fat moist lips drooling close to the microphone, repeated *ad nauseam* for a full two minutes, like some wildly insistent but unwelcome lover, the arcane injunction, ENOEST MAYDAY 7·76 SOUTH 142·4 EAST HELICOPTOUT URGENTEST MURG. It was, he later explained, precisely forty minutes short of noon in Liberia.

By now Manning and O'Halloran had picked up a little more information about their mysterious guest. He was proud to be a member of CATT, a select organization limited in number to seventy-seven. Each of these seventy-seven owned an aeroplane which he was willing to pilot to and from any two points on the globe between which a good deal might be made. Murgatreud encouraged Manning and O'Halloran to see it in electrical terms. If they would imagine two places anywhere in the world, points X and Y; and if they would then conceive of a surplus of some rare, expensive or prohibited commodity in point X and a shortage of that same rare, expensive or prohibited commodity in point Y; they would immediately appreciate that point X became, in electrical terms, positive and point Y negative; so they could readily understand the role of Murgatreud and his seventy-six colleagues with their skill, their daring and their only fractionally subsonic transport, as the electric current streaking between X and Y and resulting not so much in a flash of lightning or a clap of thunder as in another deposit in a numbered Swiss bank account.

'Is that so?' asked O'Halloran politely.

'Really?' added Manning.

'Hot ferdomma, ja,' continued Murgatreud, and went on to explain that the scheme had been started in the war by a talented character with the name of Milo Mendel. Milo had worked the racket using American Air Force transport (and he became so famous that some fellow had put him in a novel,

Murgatreud added, to underline the man's stature). But when the war ended, finding himself deprived of official support, he had set up on his own and founded CATT, the Company of Adventurers Trading Transglobe. The choice of name was a witness to Milo's romantic side. He was impressed that a famous modern firm, the Hudson Bay Company, quoted on all the stock exchanges of the world, should still use as its official title the swashbuckling 'Company of Adventurers of England Trading into Hudson Bay', and he had decided to cap them.

The organization, Murgatreud continued, with the relentless enthusiasm of a professional describing his profession, was like a co-operative of radio-operated owner-driver taxis of the air with Milo as managing director. Milo had chosen and hired the Contact, the man who passed vital messages within the group and who went on the air every day between 10.00 and 14.00 hours his time. Each member of CATT knew that if there was any message for him, any task, request, lead-in or tip, the Contact would broadcast it on an agreed H.F. Single Side Band wavelength at a certain number of minutes past noon, his own special and precise time; and exactly two hours earlier, at the same precise number of minutes past ten, the Contact would have been listening to receive any incoming message from that same member. Any of the seventy-seven who happened to be flying during those four hours would tune in for the whole period, and if they picked up a transmission that was weak through distance or atmospherics, they would relay it on. Murgatreud's time was 11.20 in, 13.20 out, but this was Liberian time, because the fleet of aeroplanes was registered for tax purposes in that land of freedom. For similar reasons all board meetings of the Company took place in the Bahamas, each member had a numbered bank account in Geneva (the Contact had the number for paying in, but only each individual member knew his own number for drawing out), and Milo had managed to get himself registered as a creative artist and was living tax-free in Dublin. The Adventurers were truly transglobe in their adventure.

'What's ENOEST?' asked Manning.

'Expense No Object, E.N.O., ja so, very much so, or not so, -est like in best, E.N.O.est, ENOEST, expense very much no object,' explained Murgatreud, adding, so much later that it sounded like self-congratulation, 'superlative.'

'And what's MAYDAY?' said O'Halloran.

'Mayday, help me, French, m'aidez, any schmuck know so, na?'

'*Aidez-moi,*' said Dr Manning.

A little less than two hours after sending his mayday message, Murgatreud tuned in his receiver. In the jungle glade it was nearly midnight, long after the bedtime of Manning and O'Halloran. But in Liberia it was 13.16. At 13.17 there was a long and elaborate message for another member of CATT about an exchange project involving pesetas and yens and the option on a load of Arctic seal pelts. 'Chickenfood,' commented Murgatreud, hunched over the set with his ear-phones. At exactly 13.20, a precise two hours after his own transmission, came the reply. It was considerably more brief. MURG WILCO.

He tugged off the ear-phones and turned to his two new friends, who with considerable difficulty had stayed awake for this unique event. 'Wilco,' he said to them, rippling all over with the excitement of relief, of contact with his own world. 'Wilco, means will co-operate, means will co-ordinate, means will collect, means wilco, wilco, WILCO,' he yelled up into the jungle night, shredding as he babbled a new pack of gum to celebrate. And, 'phop', from a fat mouth filled like a pop-gun with pressure, he sent the previous pack, a grey gob drained of all taste, spinning away into the darkened rim of trees.

14

IV

Throughout the next day, waiting for the midnight transmission which would bring details of the rescue operation, Murgatreud remained in a state of high euphoria. He told Manning and O'Halloran more about the operations of CATT. Considerably more. All day.

The Englishman and the Irishman received the news in silent wonder. They were overwhelmed by the sheer ebullience of their guest. But also the very presence of such a creature, his intrusion into their clearing, was enough to reduce them to silence. As each business deal, each rich mercantile memory was unfolded to them in its uniquely intricate beauty, they nodded and stared. Murgatreud had no objection to a quiet audience, but he was surprised, amazed, 'Hot ferdomma, flabbergast,' that they had not even heard of some of the more distinguished members of CATT. Of Henry Lyman, an early member, long since dead, who slipped up badly in Vienna? Not a word had come their way. Of Gascoyne, who once had big things going for him in the Nevada desert, and who had then joined CATT flying what could only be described as a tumbledown jalopy of the air with which he had looped the loop through the struts of the Bay Bridge at 'Frisco? They hadn't heard of anyone of that name. Of Bcn Subtle and Solly Face, who specialized in ferrying rare charms and precious potions from the remotest corners of the earth to the secret hidey-holes of the rich, and who once concocted a bespoke broth of dissolved pearl, tongues of carp and camel's heels for an epileptic millionaire? Nothing. The tall doctor and the amenable priest continued to stare at their guest in something approaching a stunned silence.

It was not only the oddity of his interests, the strangeness of his friends. It was not only their difficulty with his language, which was like a slangy international telegraphese, a mosaic of cosmopolitan fragments set in a flat ground of Brooklyn,

15

with every sentence striving for the compressed perfection of a cable, the form of communication presumably nearest and dearest to his entrepreneurial soul. It was above all that they had got to know him in the reverse order, the precise opposite of what is normal in polite society. They had intimately observed this man naked before so much as saying how-do-you-do to him clothed. Now, when he was trying to engage them in something approaching normal adult conversation, they felt in possession of a secret beyond their due. They found themselves uncomfortably aware at all times of the enormous fleshy form which they knew, by precise experience, to be lurking beneath the nylon flying-suit. With a normal person, the secret would not have seemed shameful, would have seemed not even a secret. Manning and O'Halloran could both, if absolutely required, imagine a normal person naked under a normal person clothed. But Murgatreud's shape, an obscenity in itself, was clearly a secret, and they had stolen it from him while he was unconscious. Every time they looked him pointedly in the eye, they felt that they were avoiding the rest of him. And every time they looked pointedly at the nylon flying-suit, they felt they were looking through it. They kept strangely silent.

Admittedly, meeting him socially had modified slightly their first impression of his flesh. They now saw that he was not so much the normal type of fat person or someone who had, in his entirety, swollen. He was more a man on whom the flesh had encroached. There was something firm among the pink billows which were all of Murgatreud that met the eye. He was like a rocky landscape long ago silted and clogged with rich alluvial soil which has almost buried the sharp edges. His eyelids puffed and drooped around his eyes. His two buttocks, as they knew to their shame, were squashed tight together by the sheer ambitions of each, till the cleft had been reduced to a thin straight line like half a cross scored on an unbaked bun. And now they saw that even his gums seemed to be invading his teeth, developing a soft drape of flesh between themselves and the inner lip so that when he smiled it was as if pink curtains were raised to reveal his surprisingly well-kempt teeth. But within this undulating landscape there was still visible the thin Murgatreud, the original craggy entrepreneur of the days before the numbered bank account. And he was far from being the traditional thin man screaming to get out. The very opposite. Looking down between Murgatreud's pink lids, one could see him in there, and he was twinkling with pleasure at this comfortable home he had found for himself. A tough operator concealed within a soft exterior, he was like a hermit crab in reverse, but the system of camouflage was equally appropriate. Inside and out, Murgatreud was clearly delighted with the arrangement.

V

When the Contact came through late that night, twenty-four hours after his original MURG WILCO, he was likely, thought Murgatreud, to send news of imminent rescue, probably a helicopter sortie from Port Moresby on the New Guinea coast; expensive, admittedly, but this was an ENOEST MAYDAY call, a once-for-all shot. As it was to be his last evening, Manning and O'Halloran decided to throw something of a supper party.

The table was in the space in front of the three huts. It seemed to be covered with Teresa's chequered skirt, but this was in fact the other half. Two chairs and an up-ended box were arranged on three sides of the table, and the two complete sets of knife-and-fork-and-spoon were shared out as knife and fork, spoon and fork, knife and spoon, to make three place settings. Sections of banana leaf, cut across at the broadest part, were to serve as plates.

Manning was the first to emerge from his hut. He wore a broad-lapelled dinner-jacket, bought in Singapore after the war. In parts of the world more fashion-conscious than this jungle clearing, such a garment had in the intervening twenty years gone out and come in again. It was now once more the very thing in moderately up-to-date circles, poised between trendiness and caution, but in Manning's case the effect was spoilt by the green mildew which had finally settled in, after strenuous brushing by J.K., as a pale grey patina extending in large irregular blotches over the fabric. The black bow-tie, large and floppy and, like the coat, back in fashion, had frayed at the centre from constant re-tying. The *piqué* shirt with detachable collar had lost its crisp bobbles after repeated washings in the river, and on Manning's scraggy neck the collar itself, lacking starch, now drifted apart from the shirt to form its own arc between front and back stud, revealing on each side a crescent of chicken's-neck flesh. The whole outfit testified to regular use in trying conditions.

O'Halloran was in the cassock in which he had greeted the arrival of the unconscious Murgatreud. And Murgatreud, whose suitcase of personal effects had presumably shattered in the crash, was still in the blue nylon flying-suit.

The guest of honour had a chair and the knife and fork. Manning had a chair and the spoon and fork. O'Halloran, as befitted a humble priest, had to make do with the upturned box and a knife and spoon, a combination which was likely to involve the use of fingers. '*In nomine Patris, et Filii, et Spiritus Sancti,*' intoned O'Halloran. 'Amen,' said Manning. And all three settled down.

Teresa had been cooking at a fire about thirty yards away, and now J.K. performed with considerable skill as butler. On a large banana leaf on his left hand was a pile of barbecued ribs of bush pig. On a large banana leaf on his right hand was a mound of baked yams. In traditional fashion he lowered first one leaf and then the other over the left shoulder of each guest, murmuring as he did so, 'Barbecued pig, sir,' and 'Yam, sir.' And then he placed in front of each of them a complete coconut, with holes pressed through two of the three eyes.

O'Halloran courteously took a drink straightaway, to demonstrate to the guest how a jet of the milk could be poured through one of the holes into the mouth, like wine from a leather bottle in Spain.

Through all this, Murgatreud had been droning on about CATT – about Tino Ardizzone and the priceless scarab, about Wagner's fiasco with buttermilk, about Pug Gallaher, Spotty Williams and the dare-devil Spunk – when suddenly he seemed to be struck by the distant memory of some oft-repeated instruction. He banged the butt of his palm three times against his forehead.

'Verboten natter hundred per cent number one,' he rebuked himself; and then, the positive side of the principle, with a warm smile round the table, 'So what in gottes himmel you two schmucks doin' inna hole like dis?'

Father O'Halloran smiled modestly. 'Twenty years it is that we're here now.'

'Onda run?' asked Murgatreud.

'Certainly not,' said the priest. And challenged, as it seemed, to justify themselves, the pair of hermits lost their reticence and explained how they came to be where they were. Murgatreud's attention, now that he had made the gesture of expressing interest, appeared to return exclusively to the ribs of pig and the yams, and to the diced papaya served in its own skin on the side, but from time to time he grunted his amazement in a variety of outlandish expletives.

O'Halloran had sailed from Dun Laoghaire one January day in 1947, sent by the Little Brothers of Mercy to join their mission on the south coast of New Guinea, in the small township of Kikori. He was twenty-two. He was seized with a burning desire to bring to savage peoples the message of Christ's love for them.

'Mamma mia,' said Murgatreud.

Manning had also found himself at Kikori, but he had made his way there by a more complicated route. A few years older than O'Halloran, he had graduated in 1944 from a London medical school and had been posted in the R.A.M.C. to India. Three years later, by the time that he was due for demob, his unit had moved to Malaya; and back home an ungrateful nation, or a bunch of ignorant oicks and yobs, as Manning and his friends at the time put it, had voted Churchill out and the levellers in. Manning prided himself on a certain unblinking honesty. He knew that the only things that distinguished him from the common man were his background and the pecular shape of his vowels. These, he assumed, were now to count for nothing. There was little to appeal to him in the concept of equal opportunity. He decided to take his demob in Malaya, and after being issued with his brown trilby hat, his regulation suit and shoes and socks and smalls, items which he would not have worn at home but might just wear in the East, he had set off southwards for New Guinea, a land where his innate superiority over the other inhabitants would be even more evident than in pre-war England. He also had an urge to come face to face with himself in a vacuum, in the hope of catching a glimpse of his true features.

'Hot ferdomma,' said Murgatreud. It was only weeks later that they dared to ask him the meaning of the phrase. He claimed that it was the favourite expletive of the Dutch and meant 'God damn me'.

Early in 1948, in the small port at the mouth of the Kikori river, Manning had bumped into O'Halloran, who was buying provisions for a trek upstream into the mountains. The priest had been ordered by his mission to establish an outpost in the hinterland, almost uncharted territory, and to return in about twelve months to report his progress. The idea of the expedition appealed to Manning, who offered his services as companion and doctor. By canoe for two hundred miles, and then clambering up rocky waterfalls and ravines in the higher reaches of the river, where it ran almost dry through dense jungle, the two Europeans and their dozen or more native bearers had unwittingly penetrated the territory of the New Guinea pygmies. Discovering this, the bearers – Papuans from the tribes in the plains – became reluctant to go any further. There were tales of cannibalism.

'Oi veh,' muttered Murgatreud.

'As far as we can tell, the rumours were at least a generation out of date,' commented Manning.

'So be it, inshallah,' said Murgatreud, raising five fat fingers sticky with the juice of papaya.

So the doctor and the priest had been deserted by their bearers, and O'Halloran was ill with malaria. Death seemed certain in these primitive regions. Manning, he now recalled, had been pleasantly surprised by his own calm reaction to the prospect. Perhaps his inner features were not as ugly as he had feared.

But, miraculously, the helpless pair had been taken in and virtually adopted by the tribe of pygmies with whom they had lived ever since. The precise reason for this generous hospitality was still not fully clear. But there was some suggestion that Chief Alalo's father had had a dream about the arrival of friendly strangers.

'One may not need to look hard to see the hand of God in that,' said O'Halloran, adding, as if to recognize a *fait accompli*, 'feel free with the papaya.'

They had been housed and fed. O'Halloran had recovered his health and the doctor's stock of antibiotics and pain-killers had, while they lasted, been a source of great benefit, and seeming magic, to the tribe.

Three months after their arrival, a young woman had died giving birth to twins. At the best of times twins were regarded in the community as ill-omened, and with the mother dead they were about to be smothered and buried without further ceremony. As their first practical piece of mission work, the two Europeans had adopted the children.

The boy was J.K. His education and upbringing had become Dr Manning's special passion, and he was named after an Etonian hero, J.K.Stephen, a semi-legendary figure whose name had dominated Manning's schooldays. An annual toast was drunk in College at Eton to the memory of the original J.K. and his one prodigious achievement – towards the end of the nineteenth century, while playing the Eton wall game, he had remained kneeling on the ball for twenty-seven and a half minutes in spite of the efforts of the entire opposing team to budge or crush him, a feat which in the peculiar conditions of that game was regarded as wholly admirable. Manning, whose schoolboy ideals had remained with him virtually unchanged into adult life, had devoted all his energies in the jungle to giving this tiny black J.K. the very best that the traditions of Eton could, in the circumstances, provide. Hence, for a start, the immaculate Oxford accent with which J.K. had so startled the semi-conscious Murgatreud.

His twin sister Teresa had fallen under the more relaxed influence of Father O'Halloran. She was named after Saint Thérèse of Lisieux, affectionately known as The Little Flower, a Carmelite nun who had died at the age of twenty-four in 1897, having apparently distinguished herself only by housework and obedience. But her autobiography, found and published after her death, proved a document sweet, almost sickly, in its childlike innocence. It became a runaway best-seller in the Catholic world and had been a favourite book in O'Halloran's boyhood home. And the choice of name for the tiny black orphan girl proved apt. Little Teresa had been trained to carry out every domestic chore around the white men's compound with unfailing patience and good humour. No Mother Superior could have asked for greater devotion.

So the little family grew up with a social split down the middle which reflected the origins of the two adoptive parents. J.K. was like a half-portion African prince, stamped in the mould of Eton and the Brigade of Guards. Teresa was a diminutive Irish skivvy with a sooty face.

Murgatreud's original question was still only half answered, but he now showed no sign of making further inquiry. After his enormous meal he sat slumped in his chair, totally still, in marked contrast to his normal air of bustle. It was as though a snake had just finished its monthly meal, rather than a man his supper. A faint but fixed smile linked his two puffy cheeks, as he stared across the table with unfocused eyes. But Manning and O'Halloran were in no mood to be deterred by mere lack of interest.

Why were they still here, they asked themselves? That's an interesting question, they replied. And they were willing to attempt an answer.

After their arrival, the river – the one which could be seen at the bottom of the hill, tumbling and roaring over its waterfall – had changed from an almost dry bed into a torrent. And a torrent it had remained ever since. By a lucky, or perhaps unlucky accident, Manning and O'Halloran had climbed up its bed into the mountains during a freak drought. Week by week they had at first confidently expected the river to dry up again; now they doubted whether those unusual conditions would be repeated in their lifetime. The only other way back to civilization was by cutting a path through the jungle. After the first year, and very little progress with the mission, it hardly seemed worth an arduous journey just to put in a negative report to the Little Brothers of Mercy in Kikori. Later, O'Halloran knew that the Brothers would assume him to be dead, so why spend weeks chopping through the tangled undergrowth with machetes just to inform them they were wrong? As for Manning, nobody knew that he had come, nobody would notice that he had not returned. Both men enjoyed their strange status, two oddities who had been taken under the wing of the pygmy tribe, and meanwhile there was the fascinating business of bringing up J.K. and Teresa. They felt they owed something to those who had adopted them; they owed even more to those whom they had adopted. They had a place here, a definite position.

'As if two poor wandering friars had settled in an Irish village in the olden days,' explained Father O'Halloran.

'Two Universal Aunts might be more the case,' said Manning.

These modest self-assessments clearly rounded off the saga. There was a pause. A long pause. Silence. Even to Murgatreud in his pleasant post-prandial stupor the message filtered gradually through that something was required of the audience.

'Savages,' he said.

It was sufficient.

'Not at all,' said O'Halloran, 'far from it, these pygmies have a culture of their own, I'll show you,' and he hurried into his hut.

'You'd be surprised,' said Manning.

O'Halloran came straight out again with something in his hand. He sat down on his upturned box, leant his right elbow on the table, and – smiling with some excitement – held an object towards Murgatreud's face as if shining a light into the bleary eyes of the overfed entrepreneur. Murgatreud seemed to focus with some difficulty, but the object held his gaze. Then his spine tensed. It softened its pressure on the back of the chair, there was a gap between the two. Murgatreud was suddenly on top executive form.

'Hot doggetty,' he said, 'etwas a trinket.' And he held out his hand for it.

It was circular, about four inches in diameter. It consisted of an outer band, apparently of thick gold wire, roughly beaten and showing the marks of the hammer. From this rim, strips of flat gold leaf ran towards a smooth blue mottled stone in the centre. It was like looking at the underside of a golden mushroom which had been cut from a turquoise stem.

'Gold?' asked Murgatreud, in disbelief. 'Echt gold? Like for real?'

'Of course,' said Manning, 'but not real turquoise. Just a pretty stone from the river.'

'Gold in New Guinea?' He shook his head. 'Don't figure.'

'Certainly.' For the first time, offered his favourite role of school-teacher, Manning came into his own. Gone was the hesitancy and self-deprecation with which he had outlined his part of how they came to be here. In the quiet and measured tone which J.K. knew so well from his endless lessons, the doctor enlarged on the incidence of gold in New Guinea.

'Certainly, yes, there is gold in all the rivers of New Guinea. Not enough for a European to make the sort of living he expects, though some have spent many hard years panning in the lower reaches of this same Kikori river before they finally left in disillusion. But for the pygmies it is different.

For generations they have washed in the river, fetched water from the river, relaxed by the river. Every time one of them goes down, he sifts a few handfuls and brings back any dust he may find to the tribe. And once enough has been collected, it is wrought into one of these images.'

Murgatreud had picked up the golden pendant (there was a small ring attached to the rim, to hang it from a chain). His pudgy fingers ran over the finely wrought surfaces like antennae.

'Once the new image is made,' Manning continued, 'it is taken to a secret treasure-house in the jungle, where it joins all the others made by the tribe over the generations.'

Murgatreud's lower jaw sagged. 'More now, ya tellin me?'

'Dozens. If not hundreds.'

'So? Dozens so? Like so?'

'Oh dear me, no, not like that one, no,' cut in O'Halloran. 'Indeed not, I'm sorry to say. Of all the ones we've seen, and after all these years we have seen many, but of all the ones we've seen, wouldn't you say, Manning, would you not say, that that was the only one worth having?'

Manning looked dubious at quite such a generalization. Murgatreud was frankly suspicious.

'So wasso wrong widda uddas?'

'Oh,' said O'Halloran, 'the others you see, well how shall I say it, well you know how it sometimes is with this type of people, the tribal type of people, they were for the most part ... somewhat ...'

'They were phallic,' said the doctor.

'So is dat so?' said Murgatreud.

'And huge,' said O'Halloran.

'So is dat so?' said Murgatreud.

'Huge in that respect,' explained Manning, 'rather than huge overall. O'Halloran means that there was exaggeration in the phallic region. A common characteristic, of course, of primitive art. Whether motivated by wish-fulfilment or considerations of sympathetic magic is a matter of some interest.'

But not to Murgatreud. He had no time for the scientific niceties of the case. He had dropped the circular pendant on the chequered cloth. He was pressing the crook of both thumbs against the edge of the table. He looked poised, the whole mighty bulk of him, to spring out of his seat. His eyes drilled into Manning.

'Phallic, ja?' he asked.

'Decidedly.'

Murgatreud swivelled his gaze to O'Halloran.

'And huge, ja?'

'Enormous.' And the priest hung his head.

Murgatreud gazed above the two of them deep into the dark of the jungle.

'And gold?'

'Oh yes, indeed,' said O'Halloran.

Murgatreud raised his right fist and seemed to swing it in ecstatic slowness above his shoulder before bringing it down on to the table with a crash that made the pendant jump a good two inches.

His great face followed his fist down near to the table, and he grinned up at his amazed hosts. Then he opened his palm again to the sky and flicked with his fingers, as if splashing water into his face. 'So c'mon,' he said, 'gimme a dekko, when does a fella see?'

They stared at him. O'Halloran edged the pendant out of harm's way.

'Hot ferdomma, wottawe got here?' Murgatreud went on. 'Dumbclucksville? Mamma mia, wottaya, two schmucks, dunno nuttin? Itsa goldmine, no comprenny? Itsada woiks.'

'Oh no,' said Manning, 'I fear you've misunderstood, it would involve very laborious panning in dangerously rapid . . .'

Murgatreud held a clenched fist out towards them, then raised one pudgy finger. 'Primitive,' he said, 'right?' A second finger joined it. 'Phallic, right?' And a third. 'Gold.'

He leant forward and moved his three fingers slowly, like windscreen-wipers, between his eyes and theirs.

'Crystalballtime,' he said dreamily. 'I see dealin-n-wheelin. Noah little place nayma Tiffany's Fifth Avenue, mebbe? Noah little place nayma Sotheby's, howbowdat? Or gay Paree.

Moosay Dellomme, little place one corner Palayda Chaillot, hellwidat, one corner, gimme dahole goddam Palay, all fulla echt, cordon bleu, no kiddin, twenty-four carat golden pygmay pricks, howbowdat, hey?'

He brought his fingers to rest in front of his own face, and stared through them at Manning and O'Halloran.

'Anfa why? So I tellya. Fa primitive. Fa phallic. Fa gold.' On each of his three key-words he had folded a finger. Now he held the fist out again towards his hosts, and began to move his fingers as if kneading an imaginary ball of dough.

'No comprenny up hermit creek? Primitive. Phallic. Gold.' Suddenly he flung his palm open between them. 'Swiss francs,' he said. He always thought in the currency of his numbered bank account.

'Do I take it,' asked Manning in his most precise tones, 'that you are contemplating trade of some kind with these golden images as the commodity?'

'Hey professorey, ya twigged, ya finally twigged.'

'I am afraid, then, that you have got hold of very much the wrong end of the stick. These things are not easily come by. They are used only in the sacred house, a large building in the jungle where the men of the tribe meet twice a year. It was ten years before O'Halloran and I were allowed to attend such a meeting, and another six before Chief Alalo did us the signal honour of inviting us to choose any one of the images to keep for ourselves. Owing to his higher principles and sensibilities, I left the choice to the Father.'

Manning's eyes moved from O'Halloran's face to the pendant, safely on the far edge of the table from Murgatreud. 'You see there the only example in private hands.'

But Murgatreud was not to be put off by such defeatist talk. 'Loada balloney,' he said, 'ya know da trouble wid you two schmucks?' He leant forward confidentially. 'So I tellya. Ya not pushy.'

'Really?' said Manning.

'No kidding. Fifteen years eine kleine trinket? Raus dat guy, raus. So wadya bring? Beads? Mamma mia, ya bring beads?'

'Beads, small mirrors, twists of baccy,' said O'Halloran, 'the usual.'

'Ay ay ay,' said Murgatreud, 'Queen Victoria 'n da flat iron. Old hats.'

'The Lord forgive us, the dross we lugged up the dry river bed twenty years ago, and none of it needed,' mused O'Halloran, lost briefly in his own memories.

'Beads, nix,' said Murgatreud. 'Jes leevita me, get us a deal. Buona notte, amigos, 'n sleep tight,' and he lumbered into his hut.

Manning was too discreet for any more direct comment, but he raised an eyebrow high at O'Halloran across the supper table. 'Sleep tight, then,' he said.

But any tight sleep that might have begin was effectively interrupted at 9.50 p.m., twenty minutes past eleven in the morning in Liberia, when Murgatreud began to growl into the jungle glade, lips close as ever to his microphone, a revised version of the instructions to his Contact made exactly twenty-four hours before. The new message, repeated again and again up to his full two minutes, went, CANCEL MAYDAY CHUTOUT COSTCONSCIOUS ONE THOU HAMLEYS MIXBAG MAXKIDDYJOY MARKERDEVICE THIEFPROOF MAXUNIT TWENTY-KILO MURG.

When the acknowledgment MURG WILCO had come through two hours later, Murgatreud spread his folds gratefully over the low bamboo bed and snuggled himself to sleep, warm in the comforting knowledge that he was in business again.

VI

As the thousand Swiss francs' worth of toys from Hamley's were to travel COSTCONSCIOUS rather than ENOEST, there was a delay of nearly two weeks before their arrival. Murgatreud was not idle. Indeed, he was a whirlwind of energy. The appearance of the little encampment changed more in ten days than it had in ten years. Now that he knew this was to be his base during one whole operation, he was willing to move heaven and earth to make it half way habitable. 'Let's getta bitta lebensraum round here,' he said, 'kinda hiltonize this icky dump.'

The pygmies were still sufficiently interested in him to crowd around all day, and he put them to work. The jungle was cut back into neat straight lines round the three huts in their small clearing. Paths were laid out, framed and identified by rows of pebbles from the river, to join the three huts to each other and to the communal area in the centre, where stood the table, the two original chairs and now a great basket-chair, with supple seat of woven vine, which Murgatreud had designed for himself according to the latest ideas for lounging in the West. Instead of banana leaves on the ground, Murgatreud's hut now had what was virtually a parquet floor, composed of zig-zag lengths of thick bamboo, and once he had taught two pygmies how to lay it he sent them on to extend the same courtesy to the doctor and the priest. On his walls he had his selection of favourites from the last five years of *Playboy*. Playmates of every size, type and colour jutted buttock or breast aggressively across the narrow room towards their rivals on the opposite wall, who jutted their own straight back. Murgatreud, who became more and more good-natured as each day passed, offered a selection of spare girls to the priest and the doctor. O'Halloran refused, explaining politely that he was content with his present decoration – a photograph, hand-tinted, of Pope Pius XII

29

meditating on the terrace of his summer residence, while at his feet there safely grazed an old sheep and two lambs. But Manning, after a thorough inspection, selected a particularly pumpkin-like beauty from Barbados, whom he then pinned face to the wall above his bed to reveal a slim young man dressed for squash.

And new huts were added to the compound. Where for years there had been but two there were now, within a month of Murgatreud's arrival, five. The third was Murgatreud's own, built while he was unconscious. The fourth was admittedly only a large bird-cage, an open framework of bamboo mesh, but it was as spacious as the huts in which the men lived.

Murgatreud had been bowled over by the variety of exotic birds, the screeching white cockatoos, the parakeets, the birds-of-paradise, which from time to time flew across the clearing or perched among the orchids at the top of the trees. He decided to set up an aviary. So far his spacious cage had in it only a parrot, caught for him by two of the pygmies, but as the founder member of the colony this bright and beady bird had a large part of Murgatreud's affection, as well as the benefit of every spare moment that he could afford it. For he was determined to teach this Adam without an Eve a useful phrase or two.

He had long ago been deeply impressed by an experience in an empty automobile showroom in Detroit. After clinching a deal for five hundred almost unobtainable Italian car-burettors, he had been left alone in the showroom for a few moments. For reasons of his own he particularly wanted to look under the bonnet of a new sports model. He had just got the catch free and was lifting the lid when a disembodied voice startled him almost out of his voluminous skin. 'Say, that's a great car,' it said with perfect inflection, yet metallic and somehow ominous in tone. Murgatreud had hastily pressed the lid shut, and turned. There was no one there. 'Sure is,' added the voice, behind him now. He spun again. From a cage set into the wall, camouflaged as the radiator grille in a large mural of a car, a mynah bird eyed him coolly.

It was, as Murgatreud had often said, the soft sell of all time, and he wanted something equally witty and reassuring from his own parrot. Whenever he could find time between one major improvement and the next, he would draw his big bamboo chair up to the big bamboo frame, put his face close to the mesh and repeat, ad nauseam, to the bewildered and lonely bird, 'Boy oh boy, sure is a swell scheme.' This, Murgatreud hoped, was to be the music of the glade as the operation progressed.

Undoubtedly the most impressive of all Murgatreud's improvements was in the fifth hut – a flush toilet, no less. From the remnants of his aeroplane, with the help of the tools in his emergency kit, Murgatreud had fashioned all the necessary parts – a cistern, a length of narrow tube, a pan, and a broader outflow pipe which dispensed with the U-bend and led short and sharp into a large two-handled tub under a covering of branches just behind the hut. Every stage from cistern to cess-tub had at first leaked atrociously, but some impact adhesive had served to fill the chinks. Manning, when construction began, suggested that there seemed little point in a flush system without running water, but Murgatreud with his global experience knew better. Had he not stayed years ago with a Maharaja in a remote seventeenth-century palace in Madhya Pradesh? In this ancient palace His Highness's father had installed a modern apartment of which the *pièce de résistance* was a marble-lined bathroom at the very top of the topmost tower. In a side turret, jutting over a drop of nearly two hundred feet, was the white marble lavatory, shaped like a throne, where Murgatreud had settled himself in exquisite comfort (the warmest of Indian woods separated buttock from stone), with his arms resting on smoothly fashioned tigers which slept to either side. Here, in this fairy palace, there had been a flush system without running water. Every morning before breakfast His Highness's servants, of the appropriate sweeper caste, carried water up from the river to the tank on the roof of the tower. And every morning after breakfast Murgatreud, just by pulling a chain, brought it tumbling down again. This was the royal arrangement which he now proudly reproduced at 7·76 South 142·4 East. Each time the toilet had been used, two pygmies came and tipped more water into the cistern at the top. And after every fifth flush half a dozen tiny serfs uncovered and staggered away with the tub at the bottom.

VII

Murgatreud and most of the pygmies were down by the river collecting driftwood. To one side of the white men's clearing, at the very edge of the jungle, now so much straighter than before, Manning sat on a fallen tree. At his feet, in a clump of low spreading ferns, squatted J.K.

'So we have to decide,' Manning was saying, 'whether Alcibiades, young, brilliant, unfettered Alcibiades, was guilty or merely foolish. And before we can decide that, we must know where, in such a case, guilt can be said to reside.'

J.K. twiddled slowly the long bright bone that pierced his nose, a habit of his when pondering. 'Can we perhaps' – he spoke slowly, seeking his way – 'take guilt to reside in intention? If Alcibiades did arrange for the faces on the statues of Hermes to be defaced on the night before the Sicilian expedition, did he do so intending thereby to demoralize the Athenian forces? And if so, why? He, after all, had been the chief advocate of the expedition and was one of the three commanders. On the other hand, if he had no such intention, or was not responsible for the mutilation, then the hysterical response of Athens, precipitating his flight, can be said to have led also to his subsequent treacheries abroad.

So these actions would become in essence *post hoc*, and there-fore perhaps nearer to self-defence than premeditated treason.'

'Excellent,' said Manning, 'quite excellent, though we must always remember that *post hoc ergo propter hoc* owes its fame to being a fallacy. One interesting point is that the Hermae consisted of square pillars tapering towards the ground, like an obelisk upside down. They had the face of Hermes at the top, hence their name. But they also had half way up on the front, projecting from the smooth stone, a phallus. They were cult objects, not unlike the golden images of your own tribe. Now Thucydides tells us that whoever defaced the Hermae that fateful night smashed their faces. But is it likely that a crowd of excited vandals would leave the phalli untouched? We may perhaps conclude that Thucy-dides, and all modern writers following him, have been guilty of a little prudishness. Remember that to analyse history cor-rectly we must be fearless in asking the right question. This was a subject I followed up for a few days in 1937 in the Lon-don Library.'

J.K. screwed up his face and looked into the tops of the trees, as if trying to recall a difficult detail.

'St James's Square?' he hazarded.

'Absolutely correct,' nodded Manning. 'The north-west corner.'

J.K. had had a unique education – the undivided attention from birth of a tutor well versed in certain precise fields – but it had been conducted on a purely oral basis. Indeed, the boy, so brilliant in disputation, was unable to read or write. Manning had decided long ago that with no books available, it was pointless for J.K. to waste time acquiring the written word. His education had consisted of eighteen years of almost uninterrupted conversation. By the age of six, not distracted like other children by the vivid but shapeless chatter of his own contemporaries, J.K. was already talking in the dry measured tones of an unusually earnest young English snob between the wars. And once he had mastered the voice, the inflection, the vocabulary of his *guru*, the pygmy and the gentleman were free to wander together at increasing ease

33

through the subjects common to those of Manning's background – or at least to those who, like him, had once won a scholarship somewhere.

Everything started from, and sooner or later returned to, the classics. But without the written word, with no copy available of Hillard and Botting's Latin Primer (invariably inked in at Manning's prep school to read Eating Primer), the emphasis had fallen less on grammar and construction than on the history and ideas of the ancient world. J.K.'s understanding of the Latin language was limited to a wide range of familiar tags, but he was remarkably well informed on the birth of democracy, the beginnings of empire, the uses of slavery, the socio-economic aspects of culture, the temptations of power, the seeds of decadence, and other such lessons as are found in parable form in Mediterranean history from 500 B.C. to a millennium later. After the classical period, his knowledge of European history tended to be more gossipy, forming a broad vista composed almost exclusively of poignant landmarks. He could place with unerring accuracy such historic moments as '*Qu'ils mangent de la brioche*', 'Let not poor Nelly starve', or 'Hard pounding, gentlemen'. He knew why Brown had been called Capability. He could list the surnames which spelt CABAL. He was aware of the fate of Shakespear's second-best bed. He even understood, though this was more *recherché* and derived from a special empathy felt in this direction by Manning, that Napoleon's poor showing at the Battle of Waterloo had been due to a grievous attack of piles. He was also reasonably *au fait* with the musical shows of the thirties, the geography of central London, and the history of the clubs of St James's Street. As for literature, he could recite all the poems, stanzas, couplets or even stray feet that Manning could remember, though these in sum total were few, and he had a fair grasp of the broad trends all the way from Courtly Love to Naturalism. Manning had even, without condescension, without a trace of embarrassment, more with the faint quickening of the pulse which accompanies mild flirtation, outlined to him the eighteenth-century concept of the Noble Savage.

Although originally forced on him by the lack of books, Manning in no way thought of this oral method of instruction as second-best. It seemed rather a true descendant of education in his beloved classical Greece. After all, as he had often said, such a method of teaching was nothing but Socratic, even if Socrates had preferred to dispute with more than one boy at a time. Equally, the mental and physical austerity of their open-air lessons in the jungle could only remind one of Zeno lecturing in the *stoa* on the open north side of the market-place at Athens, and surely deserved the proud name of Stoic. And when the pair of them, master and pupil, sometimes wandered peripatetic together in discussion round and round the two clearings of the pygmy village, were they not in the true footsteps of Aristotle, discoursing as he strolled in the *peripatos* of the Lyceum?

But in the area of discipline Manning did feel it necessary to reinforce the methods of Athens with those of Eton. J.K. had lived his life, though without undue nervousness, under the shadow of the cane – a greener, a fresher bamboo than its desiccated cousins in the public schools of England, but visibly of the same family. Periodically, when J.K. had fallen too far short of Manning's idea of him, the man had led the boy to a tiny private clearing in the jungle that they used only for this purpose. Here the pygmy bent to grasp his ankles and his master gave him three, four or six of what he explained were known as 'the best'. Manning confessed to himself, and even to O'Halloran, that he felt a sort of excitement in his own body as he performed this painful duty, and the excitement was heightened by the sense of ceremony. He recognized that this derived from his own schooldays, where the rituals surrounding a caning had given it an almost obsessive interest. Only extreme distinction at public schools is rewarded with the right to cane other boys. Manning never reached such dizzy heights, but in his last term he was near enough the top to watch the proceedings. He had seen the dusty pinstriped bums bent tight, had seen the fatter ones quiver slightly after each stroke. Manning was aware that J.K.'s pinched black buttocks, strangely angular and with the back of his breech-clout a mere narrow strip of cloth between them, were far from the image of his youth; but he also recognized that he was all too willing to make do with them. He was definitely ashamed of his own interest in what he had always liked to call by its proper name of *glutens maximus* – the fleshy muscle at the top of the back of the thigh which, as even the *Encyclopaedia Britannica* freely admits, 'plays a great part in determining man's outline'. To Manning's considerable relief, his mild obsession began to fade when J.K. was little more than twelve, but by a cruel irony his attention remained resolutely pinned to the same part of the anatomy. His declining interest in chastisement coincided almost exactly with the onset of his piles. His whole life, as he confessed wryly to Father O'Halloran, making the most of the shared Latin backgrounds of Eton and Rome, seemed to have been *a priori* directed *ad posteriorem*.

Manning had taken very little interest in Teresa. Her education had been left to O'Halloran, with the result that she spoke with a soft Irish brogue, and her mind was full of a medley of indistinguishable martyrs suffering tortures of infinite variety. She wore improvised Western clothes, to the extent of table-cloth skirt and bandage bra, because every Sunday (or what O'Halloran had taken to be Sunday until the date-window on one of Murgatreud's watches revealed that over the years he had let slip a couple of days, and was by now feeling extra-devout every Tuesday) she joined the Father at Mass. And, as he explained to her, it was important to preserve the common decencies in the sight of the Lord.

J.K., by contrast, went as nearly naked as any other member of his tribe and wore the outlandish ornaments of shell and bone which they regarded as elegant. Manning deliberately encouraged his dual personality, and had always insisted on the boy mixing with the tribe for a part of each day. A genuine pygmy with an understanding of Plato was what Manning hoped he was creating, not just another classical scholar more freakish than most in appearance. Thus J.K. would in the future be capable of leading his people along straighter paths. It was the concept by which the British taught Indian princes fair play and fives in the cool mountain air of Dehra Dun and then sent them down again into the steaming plains of their own ancestral kingdoms to spread the good word.

Alcibiades and his intentions had been followed from Athens to Syracuse and from Syracuse to Sparta, when Teresa approached the study group from the direction of the huts. She gave a little bob of a curtsey to Manning and coyly lifted a corner of the table-cloth.

'Excuse me, sir, but Father says Mr Murgatreud, sir, is coming up the hill, sir, and should you not all soon be ready to eat, sir, he says.'

'Tell him we're coming, Teresa.' He turned to J.K. with a concluding gesture, as if shutting the non-existent books. 'Enough for this morning, then. Good work, though, good work.' And they strolled together towards the huts, where J.K. would change to another of his roles, that of butler.

'I have the impression, sir, that Mr Murgatreud is none too well versed in the classics,' said J.K.

Manning tried, though not too hard, to conceal a smile of pleasure and assent. 'I suspect perhaps not. You may well be right.'

'When I was helping Teresa to dust his playmates, he seemed entirely to fail to take a reference I made *en passant* to the Sabine women.' Manning smiled again. The boy was as priggish as anyone about the exclusive accomplishments of people with his own background. And quite right too.

VIII

There had been a certain amount of tension between Murgatreud and his two hosts. On the morning after seeing the golden pendant, he had emerged from his hut in a state of high elation. He had chattered his way through breakfast as if somehow avoiding an obvious central topic, like a man about to propose marriage who knows that he will be accepted and enjoys the sweet conspiracy of delay. But finally Murgatreud stuffed an entire banana into his mouth, shoving in the butt end as one might force a carrot into a juicer. He pulped it with his tongue and cheeks alone, slithered it down his gullet, then leant back and squashed his palms together. At last came the question.

'So when does a mensch getta dekko?' He beamed round the table. 'When does a fella getta see da merchandise?'

'What merchandise?' asked Manning primly.

'C'mon, prof, who ya pullin da wool? Primitive phallic gold, when's dekkotime?'

'Well, did it not take us ten years to see it, keeping quiet the while,' ventured O'Halloran, 'and we had not thought, surely, you would be wanting to stop that long.'

Ten days was more what Murgatreud had in mind, or just as soon as the toys arrived – in the certain appeal of which he had the most profound faith. Manning and O'Halloran explained that he did not understand the primitive mind. Such haste was out of the question. Murgatreud in turn accused them of not having woken up to the full extent of their own influence.

'Wakey wakey, schmucks, ya on da inside, lean a bit,' he purred.

Anyway, they retaliated, what was the good in a man of action like himself just seeing the merchandise? There was no question of his being able to acquire a piece. That was a special honour which had been conferred only once by the tribe.

'Loada crap, don't gimme dat,' he replied. 'Wheelin-n-dealin, leevita me, dats a row I hoe regular. Dahole tooty-frooty caboodle, leevita me.' And he went on to ask what right they thought they had to prevent the world seeing and admiring the exquisite art of this talented pygmy people.

'Wotta we got here?' he said. 'Like, mebbe, da Mona da Lisa of dahole pygmy world, like, mebbe, right?'

38

'I suppose it could be said . . .' ventured one of the Britishers.

'Incognito. Nobody never saw but three,' and he gestured round the table, 'one, two, three, 'n finito, right?'

'Well, of course . . .'

'Europe getsa glimpse, bonanzaville, bouleversay, arse over tip, right?'

'It entirely depends . . .'

'U.S.A. raves, a wow, sperience ovva lifetime, right? Masterpiecetime, chay doeuvre, right?'

'Undoubtedly the quality . . .'

'Pygmies in, Beatles out, cover of *Time*, roll over Leonardo, na?' Murgatreud paused on this image of pygmy fame, then continued in more sombre tones. 'But. But. No see, no sales. No sales, wadya get? Little black bums nobody never knew, Mona da Lisa nobody never saw, jungle wins, oi veh, hot ferdomma, too much.' He shook his head sadly. He had slumped right down in his chair to do justice to this lugubrious thought.

'Oh quite, yes indeed, very much so,' said O'Halloran, 'but on the other hand . . .'

Murgatreud glared at him. 'I know you,' he said. 'Ya burn books.'

'We do not,' retorted O'Halloran indignantly, glad to be on a subject on which he held strong views, 'and we have not for centuries, let the truth be told. That is a slander on Mother Church and a slander on Ireland. Once a book is allowed in it will never be burnt, it can rely on that.'

Murgatreud looked as though he might be about to thump the table, but Manning stepped in to save his friend from controversy. Slowly, laboriously, in the dry tone which bored Murgatreud sufficiently to ease him back into his seat, he worked his way round to the point.

'Granted all you say,' he said, 'granted absolutely all you say, old boy,' and he slipped in the familiar phrase deliberately but with some distaste, 'the fact remains that it could be argued, and I'm not saying at this stage that this is necessarily an attitude which I share myself, or even one that perhaps

O'Halloran shares, I'm merely saying that it could be argued that your plan to acquire one or two of these golden totems in return for, oh yes, I grant you willingly enough that there is a *quid pro quo* of sorts, but in return for certain toys, might be said by some to be to a certain extent, and I am only saying what they might say, an attempt to, well, for example, they might say, exploit . . .'

The word had an electrifying effect on Murgatreud. From what appeared to be a deep doze, he sat suddenly bolt upright and asked in a loud indignant voice whether he was or whether he was not a fully paid-up member of the Primitive Peoples' Fund. The mere mention of such a high-sounding name (which Murgatreud had recently noticed in an article in *Time*) seemed enough to deflate the opposition. In truth, Manning and O'Halloran had now fulfilled their own personal need to voice that one word 'exploit', to air the possibility of such an opinion, and by doing so somehow to acquit themselves of the charge of negligence. Confronted with Murgatreud's energy and determination it was the most they could hope for. And now it was only a matter of time before they agreed at least to ask Chief Alalo if the entrepreneur might see the treasures.

As it turned out, the doctor and the priest had seriously underestimated the semi-divine status which was enjoyed by their guest – partly thanks to the manner of his arrival, dropping from the sky, but also because of his astounding shape and size. To the pygmies, it seemed the most natural thing in the world that their selection of gods should be shown to the only deity who had ever visited them in the flesh. Alalo was willing to bring the golden images to the sacred house in the jungle tomorrow, this very afternoon, whenever might be convenient. But Murgatreud thought that in a few days' time would be best.

'Tell da chief,' he said to J.K., 'Murgatreud has gods drop from sky few days from now, then we show.' While J.K. translated, Murgatreud watched the nodding serious face of the pygmy chief beneath his cassowary plumes, and he hugged himself with pleasure to think of the effect a bumper selection of toys from Hamley's was going to have on this simple savage.

'Man, ya gonna flip,' he said, with the broadest of smiles, to Alalo.

'I'm sorry, I don't understand,' said J.K.

'Stuff it, long as da guy knows I dig him.'

'I'm sorry, I don't understand.'

But Murgatreud was already puffing back up the village clearing to the small and slightly separate compound of the white men at the top end.

IX

The only other important development before the arrival of the toys was the strange case of Dong and Ding.

Among the many pygmies who spent all day hanging around Murgatreud, two held pride of place. One was the owner of the slice of propeller blade, a gory sliver of metal which he carried always with him, much as a badge of office. The other was his younger brother. These two became virtually Murgatreud's personal servants, his A.D.C.s. It was they who had caught the parrot. It was their sole responsibility to keep the cistern above the toilet topped up. It was they who summoned four other pygmies to help empty the waste tub after every fifth flush.

The only trouble was that the sword had completely disrupted the relationship between the two brothers. The lethal effectiveness of this weapon had become instant legend throughout the tribe. The two inches it had sunk into the enemy's skull had been extended by repetition until the wound had reached almost as far down as the last scrotal link of Murgatreud's manuscript and fevered imagination. So the bearer of the sword had only to raise it in a moment of mild irritation to send his brother scuttling to the jungle for safety.

Murgatreud, a man whose heart bled for injustice, endeavoured to put this situation right. First, out of the remains of his aeroplane, he fashioned the younger brother a shield. But this only prolonged each indignity. Again and again the couple could be seen moving at snail's pace across the clearing, one flailing forwards, the other shrinking backwards, like an endless rehearsal of a fight from stage right to stage left, until the weaker of the two was once more sheltering in the jungle. So Murgatreud made him a sword as well. Hostilities increased. The elder brother was not prepared to retreat before his junior, even though he was now less well armed, and blood had flowed before Murgatreud stepped in with a second shield.

For the first time here was parity, and each day the two protagonists could be seen face to face, belabouring, in turn, each other's shields. It was a ritual contest which fitted well with the traditions of the pygmy tribe, among whom any serious personal dispute, even between women, was fought out with heavy sticks – not in the thrust and parry of swordplay, which gives an advantage to the agile, but in a strict rota of blows to the arms, chest or back. It was considered improper to defend oneself, and a contest would continue, bash by unresisted bash, thump after thump, amid a circle of cheering onlookers, until one of the two turned to run from a falling stick or slumped to the ground exhausted.

The original shield had a rather high note when struck, something like *ding*. The second sounded lower, more of a *dong*. Thus battle would resound in the clearing, *ding dong ding dong*, with almost rhythmic regularity, *ding dong ding dong ding dong*, like a clock stuck for ever at the quarter hour. And the sound of the shields gave names to their owners. The man who had first found Murgatreud became known to the white men, and later to the entire tribe, as Dong. His younger and slighter brother was Ding. Watching them fight, O'Halloran murmured, 'It's a ding-dong battle, there's no denying it,' to the almost uncontrollable amusement of Teresa, and for ever after in the same circumstances he repeated it to please her.

But once or twice a sword would slip from a shield and inflict a cut, so finally Murgatreud fashioned – simultaneously – two breastplates which could be attached to similar sheets of metal covering the back, and two circular tubes, complete with eye-holes, to go over the head. The brothers could hardly move in their full armour, but they were enormously pleased with themselves and wore it on every possible occasion. There was little fighting now. In this state of extreme readiness, they were content to stand around in considerable discomfort but complete amity. For a day or two, Manning and J.K. referred to them rather self-consciously as Tweedledum and Tweedledee, none knew why. And Murgatreud, with interests in Australia, liked to call them his little Ned Kellys. But to everyone else they were, and remained, Dong and Ding.

X

Murgatreud listened regularly for any word from his Contact, and on the eleventh evening it came. MURG BURN TWO TO THREE AM STRIP ORANGE SPOT. It meant, apparently, that Murgatreud should light some time before 2 a.m. Liberian time his beacon, the large bonfire of driftwood which the pygmies had compiled down by the river on the only area sufficiently open for the pilot to have a chance of an

43

accurate drop on to clear ground. Two a.m. Liberian time was roughly noon in New Guinea. In a mood of almost carnival excitement, hot embers were carried down from the village fire, which was now kept permanently alight in the clearing (the normal pygmy method of fire-raising was too slow for Murgatreud – it involved twenty minutes of pulling a vine back and forth through a cleft stick, until the tormented wood set smouldering a bunch of dried leaves).

Soon, thick smoke was twisting upwards from the beacon and spinning away down-river on a strong breeze, and at about one o'clock a plane was heard. Moments later it was sighted, flying high. The pygmies leapt about, their arms above their heads, as if to reach up for the aeroplane and drag it down, and sure enough it began to circle steadily lower. Unique in the world, here was a cargo-cult which enjoyed the co-operation of those silver-bright high-octane gods, of whom Murgatreud in his now filthy flying-suit was the tangible representative on earth.

The pygmy hysteria heightened as the plane came steadily lower. But suddenly it levelled out, and pulled away from the site of the drop, presumably for a run-in. Now it was Murgatreud's turn to leap about in his own less athletic manner. He flung an ineffectual fist into the air, his face distorted with anger.

'Hot ferdomma, schmuckste of schmucks, down,' he yelled. 'Nix mountains, itsy-bitsy hills, down, how will he drop good, how will he drop good?' he asked the pygmies indiscriminately. But what they interpreted to be Murgatreud's late though fitting flush of enthusiasm only served to increase theirs, for the plane could be seen turning again now, and they leapt more feverishly than before. So Murgatreud directed his scorn back at the pilot, who had clearly decided that to fly any lower in this rugged country of twisting mountains and ravines would be foolhardy beyond the call of duty.

'Lily liver chicken liver yellow liver punk,' yelled Murgatreud up at him, 'I make you chopped liver black list bum.' At this moment, as if it were the pilot's disdainful reply, a puff blossomed from the belly of the aircraft and gradually organized itself into a large parachute with a container swinging below it.

'Short, idiot, dumbkopf, pazzo, short,' yelled Murgatreud, and he was right. The pilot, aware of his height, had dropped early, but he had underestimated the wind, which was against him. From where Murgatreud and the pygmies stood, it looked as though the precious package floated almost straight downwards – and straight into the jungle on the other side of the hill round which the river flowed. The plane climbed lazily away.

'Going to be devilish tricky to find over there, isn't it?' asked J.K., who had come down with Manning to watch the event.

But Murgatreud had complete confidence in his Contact's arrangements. Had his original message not specified MARKERDEVICE? Sure enough, only a minute or two later, the parachute was seen slowly rising again, from behind the hill into the blue sky, as if a film were being replayed backwards – except that now there was no package attached, only a thin wire. To the pygmies the whole sequence had been a miracle. To Manning and the well-informed J.K. this was the first touch of pure magic. But no marvel of science could surprise Murgatreud, particularly when it had been laid on by his Contact. Even when he discovered the precise details – helium had been released on impact to expand into cavities lining the parachute, and so make it rise like a balloon on a long lead – Murgatreud smiled only with the pleasure of having been proved right.

The consignment had landed in a small clearing beyond the hill, not far from a rival village. When at last the group reached the foot of the wire, they found the neighbouring tribe there before them. But Murgatreud had requested that the drop should be THIEFPROOF, and the Contact's solution proved effective.

The package was a huge sealed metal cube. There appeared to be no way into it, and only a crane could lift it entire. Pygmies were swarming all over it, and some had shinned some distance up the oblique wire leading to the parachute, drawn at an angle by the wind and depressed further by their weight. A warning shot from Murgatreud's automatic scattered them. Those round the container scampered away. Some on the wire slithered to safety. One or two dropped, in their surprise, from a considerable height, but seemed to run off unharmed.

The box was like a bright silvery die with large orange spots, but there were twelve spots on each face arranged in a circle. A cross rose from one of the twelve, like a mapmaker's symbol for a church with a steeple. In the centre of the circle, on each of the six faces, were large letters in electric-blue paint: MURG TWO OCLOCK. Murgatreud understood at once. The church gave the position of twelve. So two o'clock was two spots to the right, and on inspection this spot on each face was found to have been covered with a thin sheet of metal before being painted. With the help of chisel and pliers Murgatreud stripped the two o'clock spot on the most easily accessible of the six faces, like opening a tin of sardines. A cavity was revealed, and in it the end of a bolt. When this was turned, the entire side could be eased slowly from the cube. Inside were dozens of packages wrapped in brown paper and cardboard, looking to Murgatreud's happy eyes like a bumper Christmas stocking.

His specification MAXUNIT TWENTYKILO had ensured that each carton could be carried by a pygmy, but it was long after nightfall before the procession of tiny bearers had made its slow way back to the village. The goods were piled in front of Murgatreud's hut. During the rest of that evening, and throughout much of the following day, he inspected parcel after parcel. No one was allowed to see what they contained. But gasps of joy, rumbles of deep contentment, and prolonged, almost silent, quivers of mirth could be heard through the plaited walls of Murgatreud's residence. It was like an unending children's party for one in a bass register.

XI

Murgatreud breasted his way through the jungle, accompanied by Manning, J.K. and O'Halloran, *en route* for the crucial encounter. The containers had been neatly stacked outside the sacred house of the pygmies. They were guarded now by Dong and Ding, in full armour. They drummed their bare feet on the ground to welcome the white party – a form of salute which J.K. had suggested to them from his knowledge of the West – and Murgatreud, with a gracious nod of his head, approached the building.

It stood in the middle of a clearing and looked like a large upturned boat, except that the prow had been sliced away to make a wishbone-shaped doorway, closed now with hanging tendrils of vine. The walls were of the finest raffia, sleek and supple. It was a building of exceptional elegance.

A pygmy appeared in the doorway, holding the vines apart for the visitors to stoop and enter. From inside, the building seemed open to the sky. Only a framework of curved bamboo stood out stark and black, again like the ribs of a boat, supported on two rows of pillars. Over this framework the mesh of raffia was draped, and it acted, in its own scale, like a gauze in the theatre or a veil on a woman's face. From outside, with the light falling on it, it looked solid. From within it seemed hardly to exist.

The pygmies were squatting in two rows, facing inwards, along the line of pillars. At the far end, facing down the room, sat Chief Alalo. He wore his usual cassowary feathers, but his shells had been replaced by gold. A magnificent chain, made up of images of different shapes and sizes, hung like a mayor's badge of office on his naked chest. A pair of small figures, emphatically and proudly erect, hung from the elongaged lobes of his ears. Larger statues dangled above the heads of the squatting pygmies, suspended from a vine which ran

47

between the pillars, and almost every member of the tribe seemed to have an image in each hand.

But there was nothing repetitive about this profusion of golden objects. Only a very small percentage were abstract, of the type which O'Halloran had chosen. The rest were all figurative and all phallic, but they included weird monsters as well as men, and they ranged through a wide variety of styles. Some shared the arrested athleticism of Indian sculpture, others the static solemnity of the African or the flamboyance of ancient Mexico. Heads could be vacuous golden acorns with the simplest of features scratched upon them, or large hollow masks fluttering eyelashes of gold leaf round almond-shaped holes.

Apart from being largely made of gold, all that this multiplicity of images had in common was a reassuringly exaggerated phallus. Even here the variety was heart-warming. There were penises of gold – twisted, fluted, smooth or bobbly, baroque, neo-classical, cantilevered out from the image in every shape and size – but there were also penises of ebony, lovingly carved; penises of bamboo, with a tiny gold body wedged in the end of the barrel; penises of tasselled pigskin; penises of delicate bones spliced together in an open structure like the Eiffel Tower; even a penis of feathers, bound tightly for most of its length until allowed to burst free in a spray of plume for the top half-inch. The mood was of jubilation. But to a man like Murgatreud, who knew the value of things, it was as if he had been ushered into a new tomb of Tutankhamun.

The visitors walked the length of the building towards Chief Alalo, who rose to greet them and motioned Manning and O'Halloran to their usual places on either side of him. Murgatreud and J.K. remained standing. Without further ado Alalo, who knew that the whole object of the occasion was a mutual exhibition of gods, lifted the lower part of the heavy chain round his neck to place it in Murgatreud's hands. Murgatreud's fat fingers, their nails almost lost from sight in the flesh, ran gently, like feelers, over every knob and protuberance, while he murmured again and again, in an unusually soft and low voice, 'Beautiful, your majesty, jes beautiful, gee so beautiful, jeez,' and equally quietly, equally often, caught up in the mood, J.K. translated. Then Alalo gave a sign, and other pygmies unhooked some of the larger images from the vine on which they hung and brought them over to the man in the flying-suit. He inspected each with equal loving care. In the face of so much wealth, this large and powerful man had been suffused with a deep gentleness, like a member of the Mafia on his knees before the Virgin Mary. After what seemed an eternity of adoration, Alalo gave a sign that enough was enough. And Murgatreud heaved himself out of his trance – back from the golden future into a present in which he, a leading member of CATT, was solely responsible for assuring that future.

The change was electrifying. Instantly the old bustle was back. Murgatreud the operator, Murgatreud the super-salesman was on. He brought in the first of his containers (he had carefully numbered them), and Dong and Ding stood to either side as he unwrapped it. With a flourish he lifted out a bright box. It was covered in the garish diamonds of a harlequinade, and had a big brass hook and eye for a catch. Murgatreud placed his hand firmly on top of it and looked towards Chief Alalo.

'Alalo, what have we here?' he asked in sombre tone, but suddenly something amused him. A humorous thought would strike Murgatreud much like a sharp tap on a blanc-mange. Long after a good joke, ripples of merriment con-tinued to ebb back and forth in his fatty tissue. The sound of the pygmy chief's name had brought back early London memories – of visits to the music hall with his father during the long journey from Vienna to Pennsylvania, and of tradi-tional jokes about the flat-footed British bobby. The sound of the name was so easy, so convivial, so familiar that nothing could hold him now, the deal was a cinch.

'Alalo, what seems to be the trouble . . . ?' he said, vibrating with mirth as he pretended to struggle with the catch, and then, 'Whoops,' he raised his hand and a black frizzled head, grinning sheepishly at all and sundry, leapt into the air and waved about on the end of its spring. There was a moment, a fairly long moment, of silence – and then a noise of soft and flabby drumming on a solo instrument. Chief Alalo was patting his stomach with both hands in a rhythm of elementary syncopation. The rest of the tribe followed suit and there was a sound from all sides of a thousand distant raindrops.

'Like it?' asked Murgatreud, aside.

'They like it,' replied J.K.

After this there was no holding him. His principle was that of the three-ring circus – the more going on at once, the better the show. He taught Dong how to incarcerate and release the hapless golliwog, while he himself unwrapped further delights. Ding was set to work on a hurdy-gurdy, and J.K., having instantly mastered a humming-top, was soon responsible for a gyroscope as well. Murgatreud himself operated the more complicated mechanical toys. He wound up an astronaut, who plodded five laborious paces forward and then paused to atomize all who might oppose him with a shower of sparks from his ray gun; a bulldozer which scraped and shoved the dust of the ground before it; and a tin poodle, lowering from its anus a long brown thread which coiled neatly between its back legs, and then, even more surrealistically vile, sucking it slowly up again. He pumped up a rocket, which for many seconds appeared to do nothing, but then suddenly burst from its launching-pad and embedded itself in the raffia of the roof, where it remained. He set a duck dipping up and down by some chemical law into a beaker of water. He produced a little car which was designed never to fall off the edge of a table, but as there was no larger flat surface available than the lid of a cardboard box it spun like a demented mouse. He took a quick turn with a diabolo, another on a yo-yo. And he wound up again and again the Pataphysical black box, which shook itself almost to the point of disintegration, whereupon the lid slowly opened and a tiny hand emerged to switch the thing off, an allegory of Murgatreud the humourist being controlled by Murgatreud the businessman, except that Murgatreud the businessman knew his audience, or thought he did, and promptly set it off again.

And all of this to constant cries of ''Ullo, 'ullo, what have we here?' or 'Alalo, HALLO!'

Finally every toy had had an outing and the team was exhausted. Murgatreud stopped winding up the machines. The astronaut paused suddenly in mid-stride. The poodle was left with an inch and a half of brown thread dangling from its rear. Directed by some invisible superego, the pink hand emerged for the last time from the black box to suppress its own id. Soon the only remaining movement was silent – that of the duck still dipping to its water-hole. After a pause there was a positive rainstorm of polite applause as the pygmies all pattered their fingers on their bellies.

Murgatreud, selecting the black box as the most magical and significant of his gods, advanced with it towards Chief Alalo. At this crucial moment he dispensed with the services of J.K. Instinct and sign-language are sufficient all round the world for the archetypal discussion which he knew was to follow. Holding the black box on one outstretched palm, he gestured with the other to one of the images on the chief's necklace, and then moved his two hands, one empty, one full, backwards and forwards in a slow syncopation highly suggestive of milking. Chief Alalo signed that Murgatreud should sit down. Murgatreud shook his head sweetly. The chief leant back, away from the fat hands, and repeated his gesture.

'He wants you to sit down,' said J.K.

Murgatreud paused, then sat down. J.K. settled himself beside him.

Alalo eased his neck under the weight of his necklace, rearranged slightly the pattern of the ornaments as they dangled on his chest, placed his hands on his knees and stared straight down the hall. Then, impassive, he emitted a long high 'Ooooooooooooooooh,' which suddenly plunged deep into a bass register with another syllable. Swooping, hovering, rising, drifting, all with accomplished ease, like a gull on a breezy day, his sounds, presumably words, floated with great clarity down the long hall. To achieve this, his lips, his jaw, his tongue formed themselves into a series of extreme contortions of almost military precision. Each position was held for the length of one sound, then changed in a flash to the next. It was like watching a series of single frames from a film of an opera singer.

Murgatreud fidgeted. This thing seemed to be going on and on. It was like an open-ended radio programme composed entirely of atmospherics. But as suddenly, as abruptly, as he had begun, Chief Alalo stopped. He resumed his position of absolute stillness, staring down the hall.

'He says,' said J.K., 'that he thinks your gods are an awfully good show.'

Murgatreud was all smiles. He clasped his hands together above his head like a victory salute, and started to say 'Well, howbowdat, howbow . . .'

But the chief was off again. Except that this time he started on a low note, his performance seemed identical, a repeat rather than a true encore. And again it lasted far too long. When it did finally end, and Alalo was back in his impassive Buddha position, Murgatreud turned with a smile to J.K.

'But,' said J.K., 'he doesn't feel they'd be all that hefty in a crisis.'

Murgatreud's face slumped. A volcanic eruption seemed to gather force deep inside him. But Chief Alalo had broken his pose. He was pointing now beyond Murgatreud, and with a much more friendly expression was waggling his head from side to side. Murgatreud turned. The chief was pointing at Dong. Instantly Murgatreud, the businessman, understood. He needed no further consultation, was going to risk no more arias. He scrambled to his feet and wrenched the Ned Kelly stove-pipe helmet off the bewildered pygmy. Feverishly Murgatreud released the things which held the breastplate to the backplate so that he was able to hinge open the double carapace to reveal the quivering naked figure beneath. Sword and shield followed. Almost instantly the entire suit of armour was laid out in front of Alalo, neatly stacked like the trophies on an eighteenth-century tomb. The pygmy chief rose, took a golden image from one of his seated tribesmen and handed it to Murgatreud. But even in this moment of triumph, snatched from the very jaws of disaster, the fat man's business acumen did not desert him. He looked glumly, even impassively, at the precious object in his hand. After a pause the chief presented a second image, and Murgatreud's smile revealed that the deal was on.

Alalo slowly, ceremonially, removed his crest of cassowary plumes and handed them to one of the near-by pygmies; likewise the ornaments on his ears, and at last the great necklace of golden images. Then Murgatreud personally helped him into the suit of armour, until once again the little man stood proudly before his people, indistinguishable now from Dong a few moments before. A ripple of applause ran round the hall, from belly to belly.

But Murgatreud had turned to settle an urgent domestic problem. There was an explosive situation, one which had to be promptly defused, in the new disparity of armament between Dong and Ding. Ding, fully armed, confronted now an older brother as naked as a shrimp without its shell. No doubt Murgatreud's first thought was for domestic harmony as he rapidly stripped Ding of his accoutrements. But perhaps his *alter ego*, as a member of CATT, had a hand in it too.

An eerie sound, like the wind sighing in a chimney, came from the direction of Chief Alalo. Dong's helmet had eye-holes in it, so the chief had seen the second pile of armour but it had no opening for the mouth, less necessary in a subject than a king. The sound was another of Alalo's arias, another royal proclamation finding its way as best it could from inside the stove-pipe helmet. One of the pygmies nearest to the chief stepped forward and began to put on the other suit of armour.

'His eldest son,' said J.K.

Certainly Alalo assumed that the second deal had been intended by Murgatreud. Without further argument he handed over two more golden images, and after this the ceremony wound rapidly to a close. For the moment neither party to the deal had much further interest in the other. Each was more concerned with his purchase.

Murgatreud bowed his farewell to the rough tin can with two spindly legs, and then rapidly departed – leaving his gods littered all over the floor, to the considerable amazement of the pygmies.

'So how many sons old Alalo?' he muttered, as soon as they were outside the sacred house.

'Seven,' replied J.K.

XII

That night the longest message yet went off to the Contact in Liberia, specifying the delivery of a very wide range of goods. It would take weeks rather than days to gather them together, but it was a new, a calm Murgatreud who awaited them. Now that he knew for sure what he was on to, he was content to relax. He could even be seen sitting in the glade in his large bamboo chair, hands slumped on his belly, watching the work in progress. He seemed pregnant, waiting for the dawn of the future.

Thick bamboos were being felled to add another room to Murgatreud's hut. Each of the new canes was set deep into the ground, flush with its neighbour, to which it was then bound tight with vines, and the roof was to be as impenetrable as the walls. The new room was the same size and shape as the existing one, with which it shared one wall like a pair of semi-detached bungalows, but they would be ill-assorted twins, one hard and deep-rooted, the other little more than a three-dimensional trellis. It was in keeping with Murgatreud's present hopes that his safe should be as large as his house.

Murgatreud watched the work, only occasionally stirring himself to correct a detail. Dong and Ding had been promoted from the labour force and were leading an easier life. To compensate them for the loss of their armour, Murgatreud had allowed them to take on the education of the parrot. They had learnt in a minute what seemed likely to take the gaudy bird a year, and they now squatted on either side of the cage ceaselessly striving to pass on their knowledge. 'Sure is a swell scheme,' Dong would observe in an acceptable trans-Pacific accent. 'Sure is,' Ding would invariably reply. If less miraculous than the entire refrain being carried by the parrot, the effect was in the short term almost as satisfactory. As Murgatreud had always intended, the glade seemed filled with optimism.

Only one irritation briefly disturbed these happy days. It concerned part of Murgatreud's order. The relevant section of his message had run XEROX ARMOURENGRAVINGS EARLY ARMAMENTMANUALS TOPSELECTIONS WORLDLIBRARIES. The Contact's contacts were to seek out the rarest and most beautiful of early printed manuals (exquisite books, Murgatreud had bought and sold many of them himself, with deep-cut, starkly clear engravings showing the royal craftsmen of the day how to build a boat, secure a falcon, divert water over a mill-wheel or saw off a leg), and having tracked down these rarities in the more select libraries of the world, they would Xerox the plates on the craft of the armourer, with cross-sections of greaves and pauldrons, ventails, beavers and faulds, dotted with A and a and *a*, or 7 and VII, or ◊ and ✠ and ✣, signs relating to detailed accompanying instructions in any or all of Murgatreud's five fragmented European languages. These delicious objects, he assured Manning and O'Halloran, his Contact's contacts would soon be sending him.

But late one night, in the early Liberian afternoon, a message came through: GUNPOWDER PREDATES PRINTING EARLY ARMAMENTMANUALS ENGRAVINGS INVARIABLY GUNS.

Hardly had the words crackled through the ear-phones into delayed coherence, when Murgatreud flung the contraption from his head and was wrenching with both hands at scanty hair. 'Hot ferdomma wotta dumbkopf,' he yelled.

'What's up?' asked Manning, emerging from his own hut in faded pyjamas. 'Problems?'

'Know wotta dumbkopf say?' roared Murgatreud, and repeated the message.

'Most interesting,' said Manning. 'Yes. One tends to forget how early gunpowder was on the scene and how late printing. And of course Hero of Alexandria invented a sort of steam engine, as well as automatic doors for a temple, in the second century B.C. Intriguing business, the history of invention. Most.'

Not to Murgatreud. He seethed all that night and during the long next day until it was his turn to speak. Then his riposte was growled and spat out into the clear night air. ANYDATE ARMSANDARMOURMAKERS KNOWHOW CHRISSAKE SOONEST. It was rare that he was so disturbed as to waste the odd second, in each repetition of the message, on a transglobal expletive.

XIII

The second drop was far more efficient than the first, even though there were now three containers, each as large as the one which had brought the toys. The pilot flew low, and on each of three runs dropped his load into the open space by the river. The marker-devices rose, as before, but they were hardly necessary. MURG SEVEN said one container, MURG THREE another, and MURG TEN the third. He stripped the relevant orange dots.

The packages inside were of more varied size and weight than before. Some were long and flat and flexible, and seemed to develop an inner life of their own when a man tried to jog up the hill with them. Others, smaller but even more mysterious, were heavier for their size than anything the pygmies had come across. Great merriment was caused when a man stooped confidently to lift one of these, but was instead dragged by the object down to the ground, falling forward on to his face. And the joke was heightened when others had lifted the parcel on to his head and he staggered away up the hill, sagging at the knees and reeling inexplicably sideways under a bundle no bigger than a few coconuts.

Murgatreud opened each package in turn inside his hut. There were sounds of wire being snapped, staples being forced apart, brown paper being stripped, with short grunts of energy, sharp exclamation marks of surprise, slow sighs of acknowledged content, all the mixed ingredients of an orgy of present-opening.

Manning and O'Halloran sat in the glade. The event was too absorbing to be overlooked, yet their participation was clearly not required. Sometimes when Murgatreud emerged they would try and insinuate themselves a little.

'That's heavy work,' ventured O'Halloran. 'Could a person not lend you a hand with that?'

'Nana, do fine,' and he was out of sight again with another unopened treat.

'Doing fine, are you?' continued Manning on a later occasion.

'Topnotch. Squisito.'

'Well, that's fine.'

And later again, 'You're in a lather of sweat, you won't mind my observing,' observed O'Halloran. 'Should you not take it easy?'

Murgatreud made no reply, but soon after this he was out of sight for a full thirty minutes. When he reappeared in his doorway, he was transformed.

Gone were the familiar blue flying-jacket and the leather boots, lined with moth-eaten artificial fur, which Murgatreud preferred to wear unlaced. He was now in white; a white shirt with button-down pockets on each breast, and an open neck, in the narrow V of which Murgatreud swelled as plump and proud as a turkey; white shorts, voluminous and lengthy, with a reassuringly broad flap over the flies which were clearly fastened by buttons rather than a zip; white stockings up to the knee, held tight and neat and level by white woollen garters with cheeky white tassels; and in the crook of his left elbow, where cavalry officers used to carry their plumed helmets when sitting for their portrait, a spanking new white solar topee. It was a complete tropical kit, terminated at one end by the pink flush of Murgatreud's sweaty face and at the other by a pair of sensible brogues, still of the naïve and bilious colour peculiar to new brown shoes.

Murgatreud held his pose.

'I say,' said Manning, 'you've spruced up.'

'Oh indeed, it's a magnificent outfit,' added O'Halloran.

Murgatreud smiled graciously, and produced from his hut a bottle of Napoleon brandy, a tin of *marrons glacés* and one large bulbous brandy glass. He joined the others at the table. Napoleon brandy and *marrons glacés* were his special specialties, he explained. Whenever he settled in an out-of-the-way spot, his Contact would send them. With a new penknife, on which a corkscrew was only one of some twenty fittings, he uncorked the brandy. The *marrons glacés* had their own built-in key. There was only one brandy glass because the Contact had thoughtlessly forgotten his new friends. Murgatreud laughed convivially. Never mind, let it circulate.

'Hot ferdomma, wotsa bitta spit among amigos?' he pontificated. 'Love-cup, why not?' He pushed the glass with a generous helping of brandy over to Manning, the gentleman of the group, while at the same time directing the open tin of saturated chestnuts towards the priest. 'We celebrate,' he said.

'By the by, though,' said Manning, who was cradling the brandy glass in the palm of his hand, circulating it so that the brandy rode high round the walls, and who now interrupted his own awkward question to extend his nose towards the rim and inhale, and, 'Mmmmm, damn good, I must say,' he murmured, before returning to his original observation, 'but, by the by, I mean, celebrate what? I mean, exactly. I mean, for example, what exactly is in all those boxes? Don't you agree, O'Halloran?'

O'Halloran did agree. With every word. Trying to conceal the fact that his mouth was full of a *marron glacé*, he wagged his head vigorously up and down. 'Oh, definitely,' he said, and swallowed.

So Murgatreud explained with unusual gentleness, with no one branded a schmuck, with hardly a hot ferdomma, that in the packages was all the equipment for a small ultra-modern smithy with which he would fashion as much excellent armour as Chief Alalo and his warriors might require. Manning and O'Halloran had agreed, at the time of the toys, that the world should see and appreciate the beautiful golden artefacts of this talented little people. So why should they feel anything but enthusiasm now that the scheme was being so satisfactorily enlarged?

'On the other hand,' said Manning, 'it does seem a trifle ... irresponsible may be too strong a word, but a trifle ... something of the sort ... to introduce into a peaceful village these weapons of aggression.'

'Na. Defence.'

'Every country labels its military budget Defence.'

'Peaceful? Frighten me outa ma wits, da yodel artiste.'

'Oh, we're not saying that left to themselves they're little angels.'

'But even so, you know,' put in O'Halloran.

Murgatreud passed the loving-cup. The priest and the doctor had not tasted alcohol for twenty years. When their turn came round for the brandy glass they only sipped, where Murgatreud swilled. Even so, the succession of sips was having a very pleasant effect.

'See it my way,' said Murgatreud, 'all da good'll come. Like, mebbe, how much goodya done? Numbera lives ya saved, numbera souls, twenty year, huh?'

The alcohol released the full flood of their natural modesty.

'Not much of a score, I think we'd freely admit,' said Manning. 'My friend here has taught the little fellows some hymns sort of phonetically, sound by sound, you know, and we often have a sing-song in the evening with them, they seem to enjoy

it, and anyone chancing on us then would be quite impressed,
I suppose.'

'But like numbera baptism, numbera wedding, funeral,
confession, Mass?'

'There's not been too much of that, what with the language
problem and all,' said O'Halloran, 'but my good friend here
is far and away the best doctor they've ever had.'

'Which is not saying much.'

'Oh, I wouldn't say that.'

'Admit it, O'Halloran, we're not exactly number one
mission for South-East Asia.'

'It may be that the Little Brothers of Mercy in Kikori had
hoped for more, I would say it may well be.'

'The understatement of the decade, old chap.'

'I suppose it is.'

Murgatreud had kept a respectful and sorrowing silence
during this duet, but now, with a generous wave of his hand
and a mumbled 'Grabba marron, feel free', he seemed to
sweep away the past as he eased himself gently back into the
conversation.

'So missionary guys elseplace mebbe they done better.
But for why? Had summatta offer. Soup ta offer, lodging,
aspirin, pants. Gospel comes widda soup, na? Only savages
ya had summatta offer, J.K. 'n Teresa, cent per cent, na?'

'He has turned out rather well, I do like to think,' said
Manning.

'Oh, she's a good girl,' added O'Halloran.

Murgatreud passed the brandy glass, and quietly began to
explain that at last, through him, they would have something
to offer. He outlined to them the brave new world which
would derive from his activities.

To O'Halloran he conjured up a picture of a latter-day,
miniature, black crusade. He sketched an image of rank
upon rank of pygmies, each in a gleaming breastplate with a
bold cross upon it, marching to take the Faith to the outlying
districts. O'Halloran murmured some doubt about whether
the Crusades had been entirely a good thing. But Murgatreud,
who was under the impression that they had led to the

creation of the state of Israel, would hear not a word against them.

To Manning he offered a more sophisticated argument. Only a fully primed economy could afford such sophistications as modern medicine. To primitive man war was the most inspiring of projects. The chance to buy better weapons would galvanize the pygmies into previously unsuspected energy, and from this would come the wealth to invest in science and education. The whole history of the white man's progress from savagery to the heights of modern civilization was spread out like a well-charted route-map. The little people needed only the first gentle shove and they would be able to follow that whole and happy route. Murgatreud was here to give them that shove. And he very much hoped that his two good friends would be willing to lend a hand. He circulated the brandy, which was guaranteed to contain a drop from the great days of Napoleon, and he circulated the chestnuts.

Neither Manning nor O'Halloran was in a mood to break up the party.

'We'll go along with that, why not,' said Manning.

'Indeed we will, I would certainly say, between friends,' added O'Halloran.

'In such a case,' said Murgatreud, with the smile of a gigantic cherub, but he didn't finish his sentence. He almost tiptoed away, and returned from his hut with a large cardboard box. Out of it he took a shining black cassock, a white surgical robe buttoning high round the neck, and a pair of rubber gloves. There followed some sober black trousers of O'Halloran's size, and more elegant fawn ones to fit the tall doctor. Murgatreud gestured to the two men, who sat in stupefied silence, to try them on. While they did so, he brought another box from his hut and unpacked its contents on the table. In front of the doctor appeared the complete range of drugs and instruments which would be purchased today by any young man setting up in general practice. In front of the priest there were soon four bottles of red wine a large carton of holy wafers beautifully wrapped in tasteful cardboard and Cellophane by a firm in Rome, the leading suppliers to the trade, and a bottle of colourless fluid.

'Gin, nix,' chuckled Murgatreud. 'Echt Jordan.'

Even this was not all. A school uniform, such as girls wear to convents, was now unpacked for Teresa. It was Madonna blue, with pretty white cuffs and collar, and there were two matching hair-ribbons to go with it, intended no doubt for thick dark Mediterranean plaits. These were hardly suited to Teresa, whose hair was the springy black bush worn by all the pygmies (so deep and dense that they were in the habit of storing their more precious keepsakes in its safest recesses near the scalp), but she entered into the spirit of the occasion by plunging the ends of the two ribbons into her hair so that they hung down over her shoulders in place of the plaits they were meant to adorn. There was also an Eton jacket – a complete outfit of striped trousers, white shirt with stiff collar and tie, and a little shrunken black coat – intended for K.J. This was less of a success.

'Bloody bum-freezer, is it?' asked J.K., instantly recognizing a garment familiar from Manning's descriptions of the old school.

'Now, now, none of that,' muttered Manning. 'You needn't wear it again, but you must this once, since the gentleman has been so kind.'

So J.K. put on the ridiculous garments, without removing the long white bone from his nose or the shells from his ears. There was even a mortar-board for Manning, which was intended to complement the boy's outfit. He placed it on his head above the surgical overalls.

They made a motley crew, lined up behind the table, but the fat man in his white tropical kit, the uncrowned Father Christmas of the scene, rubbed his hands with delight at what he and his Contact had achieved.

'Awfully kind of you, I must say,' said Manning.

'Oh yes, indeed,' said O'Halloran. 'And how did you get them to fit?'

'No bother,' said Murgatreud, delighted at being asked

to explain the sytem. 'Two CATT members same size, bobsya uncle.'

In fact the relevant part of the message, providing clothes for all, had run to less than a dozen words: PERSONAL MURG-TROPICAL PRIESTKIT GASCOYNESIZE MEDICO MILO UNIFORMS BOY GIRL AGE TEN. The system, Murgatreud felt with some justification, was just great.

XIV

The Contact had also sent a wide selection of books on armour. There were nineteenth-century tomes, mainly learned catalogues of individual collections, such as *Descrizione della Reale Armeria di Torino*, Turin, 1840, in which large fold-out steel engravings showed every separate piece of a particular suit of armour, laid out side by side like numbered bones from a skeleton. And there were modern glossy books (of which *Der Waffenschmied und seine Kunst*, 36 colour plates and 70 mono, Nuremberg, 1968, rapidly became Murgatreud's favourite), in which helmets, shields and breastplates were presented as *objets d'art*, photographed against tasteful matt backgrounds as if suspended in air.

Here could be seen the familiar progression from functionalism to luxury. The earliest helmets derived their very considerable beauty from the patina of long use. Like an old knife, whose handle has yielded to the palm and its blade to the stone, or like an ancient hard-worked human face, their very shape and texture stirred the imagination. Their road to the final safety of the museum had been a long and dangerous one. At the other extreme, three or four centuries later, were the helmets top-heavy with elaborate crests in silver and gold, heraldry in three dimensions, the proud mathematics of dynastic copulation advertised abroad. Each was a masterpiece of conspicuous consumption, a Blenheim Palace in miniature. These had been museum objects from first to last. Unveiled by the master armourer amid more excitement than even Master Holbein could expect for one of his portraits, they had been worn once only in the reasonable safety of the joust and had soon found an honoured place behind glass in the baronial hall.

Murgatreud also discovered, from his concise little library, the principle by which weapons develop. A manual called *Aux armes, citoyens!*, Paris, 1910, gave three stages in a hypothetical arms race.

Stage One. A and B are two rival communities, who for years have fought each other with identical weapons. They attack with a medium-length sword of the slashing variety, which requires a long heavy swing for its edge to take effect. Thus any dangerous blow must come from above, and the soldiers require protection only on the upper surfaces of the body ('*là où tomberait la neige*'). They wear simple iron hats, and chain-mail over the shoulders.

Stage Two. One day the warriors of A enter the field with a new weapon. Each man carries a sword twelve inches longer than the usual. Not only can they now outreach the cowering men of B, but with its extra weight this sword can slice through the chain-mail which until now has been adequate defence. B are ignominiously routed.

Stage Three. To re-establish themselves, B can adopt the larger sword; but this will at best restore parity, and A have acquired a confidence in the use of this particular weapon which will be hard to match. B will be wise to find a new approach. So they replace the chain-mail on their shoulders with the much stronger plate-mail, and they *shorten* their swords to something approaching a dagger, an instrument for stabbing rather than slashing. At the next confrontation, A advance confidently swinging their Excaliburs, which have already been proved invincible (a treacherous word in the armament business), and B move forward beneath the blows, unharmed, to plunge their short swords into the exposed soft underbellies of their astounded opponents.

Stage Four was left a question mark. Will A make their swords yet heavier, to the very limits imposed by human muscle, in the hope that thus they will cut through even plate-mail? Will they extend their own chain-mail downwards to counter the wicked thrusts of the dagger? Will they shorten their own swords, fix a shield to the left forearm, and go straight for the bellies of B?

Their choices are, Murgatreud was delighted to note, almost endless. He read with tears in his eyes of weapons for cutting, weapons for thrusting, weapons for prodding and crushing and puncturing, even some for prising and winkling. Seated in his large bamboo chair, not far from where Dong and Ding were educating the parrot, he browsed his way through the pile of books until his mind was filled, like a castle armoury, with gleaming rows of halberds, pikes, maces, knouts, spontoons, partizans, ranseurs, flails, miseri-cords, morgensterns, and the dreaded Holy Water Sprinkler.

The real beauty of the pattern was that A's choice is ultimately unimportant. Whatever weapon they develop it will give them at best a temporary advantage, which in turn must give way to the next temporary advantage, which will thus lead, with perfect predictability, towards the present temporary perfection of early warning systems and intercontinental ballistic missiles. Murgatreud had suddenly in his mind a clear picture of the whole progress of man, and it looked good. He was only concerned professionally with the progress of man through the Middle Ages, but it pleased him to see his own special period as part of the larger pattern. It somehow added a certain something to the intrinsic value of the scheme he had in mind.

XV

The smithy was set up in the open air near the five huts. Murgatreud mixed two small bags of sulphate-resistant cement with shale and gravel from the river, and built an open hearth by enclosing a circle, about three feet across, with a wall – much like the outer defences of an unusually ambitious sand-castle. In the curving wall he set a metal fan, turned manually by a heavily geared and insulated handle – which Dong and Ding soon learnt to spin at remarkable speed, changing from one hand to the other without breaking the rhythm, when a really hot flame was required in the forge. The remainder of the cement was used for lining a large square hole in the ground, which two days later was filled with water. Between the forge and the pool, the anvil was firmly bedded. Finally, the sheets of metal were unwrapped from their heavy brown paper and were stacked neatly beside the gleaming new tools – hammers, tongs, punches and cutting devices. And Murgatreud was ready.

The manufacture of suits of armour proved surprisingly easy. Murgatreud took as his model a twelfth-century suit from Silesia, illustrated in Plates 1–4 of *Der Waffenschmied*, which was little more than a refinement of the simple Ned Kelly outfits he had improvised for Dong and Ding. With a small oxy-acetylene torch, he was able to cut his patterns from the sheet-metal with the ease of a tailor rather than a blacksmith, and the Contact seemed to have anticipated every tiniest problem. There were even felt pads as lining for the shoulders of the finished suits, since the pygmies, unlike the knights of old, would be wearing these unwieldy husks next to the skin.

One omen seemed most propitious for the start of the new venture. Provoked by the constant din of the hammer as it bashed the red-hot sections into shape on the anvil, the parrot decided to speak up. 'Sure is,' he squawked indignantly one afternoon; and the next day, after long prompting by Dong and Ding, he was prepared to complete his statement. 'Sure is a swell scheme,' he screeched above the racket; 'sure is.' And for ever after he continued to scream his fury in these soothing words.

All the pygmies stood watching, until Murgatreud put them to work building a high palisade of bamboo round the smithy. Even while they laboured, they stared in a delirious stupor at the magic being performed in their midst – at the oxy-acetylene spitting blue fire and golden sparks as it ambled its way through a substance hard as stone, at the shapes which went black into the furnace and came out red, at the hiss and venom of the water as it restored the original black. There were to be two doors in the palisade, one giving on to the centre of the clearing, and the other, mysteriously, at the point where the enclosure bulged slightly into the dense edge of the jungle. Once they were both fitted, complete with firm wooden bolts sliding between bamboo posts, Murgatreud ushered the pygmies out into the clearing and then, to their very great surprise, locked the door behind them. They heard the fascinating work continuing within. But it was the last they were ever to see of it.

After a few weeks, twenty-five suits of armour and as many swords were ready. Each bore the red cross of Saint George on the breastplate, and a smaller cross, in gold, on the front of the helmet. The suit intended for Chief Alalo was covered in a delicate arabesque of white and blue. It was copied from the armour of Augustus, Landgrave of Hesse, illustrated in colour in *Der Waffenschmied*.

This, felt Murgatreud, was the least he could do for the old boy – because when it came to the bargaining session it was, inevitably, a seller's market. The twenty-five suits of armour and the swords were laid out in a gleaming row down the centre of the sacred house. Almost any price would have been acceptable to the pygmy chief once he had seen the finished goods. In the end, Murgatreud took the chain round Alalo's neck, four of the largest images hanging from the pillars, and an armful of the smaller images with which he had been paid before. He was relieved to see that several images were on show today which had not been brought out on the previous occasion. The gold mine was proving richer than might have been feared.

All these new images were stowed away in the strongroom attached to Murgatreud's hut. And a large padlock was produced from one of the Contact's cardboard boxes to go on its door.

XVI

Practice in the use of the armour united the community as never before. Every morning the entire tribe gathered in the village clearing for a joyous session with the three white men. Each day's programme consisted of instruction in religion, followed by study of the skills of warfare and elementary medicine, the three subjects always being taken in that same logical order. Murgatreud had made it plain from the start that the possession of the new weapons, with their bright painted crosses, was indissolubly linked with the magic of Father O'Halloran and his neo-baroque crucifix of brass. So the scripture lesson came first.

As it was impossible to sit down in the complete suit of armour designed by Murgatreud, the pygmies during their period of religious instruction wore only breastplate and helmet. Chief Alalo, together with his sons and other select warriors to the total number of twenty-five, squatted in the front row. In this state of partial transformation they were an incongruous sight. The twenty-five gleaming helmets with their smaller crosses of gold reached down to twenty-five gleaming breastplates with their larger crosses of red, which reached down to twenty-five pairs of spindly black legs, neatly crossed, like bows of dark ribbon on twenty-five tiny loin-cloths. Crusaders above, ascetics below, they were surely, as Manning dryly pointed out, the perfect images of Christian gentlemen. Behind the curving row of warriors sat the rest of the tribe, women and children as well as the hapless men who had not been selected for the armoured platoon. Every-one was determined to benefit from the magic.

Father O'Halloran, resplendent in his new cassock, stood facing the semi-circle in the jungle clearing. Beside him stood the brass crucifix, now attached to a bamboo pole. The lesson consisted mainly of stories about Jesus Christ, stories designed to demonstrate His meekness, His quality of long-suffering, His willingness to turn the other cheek. O'Halloran was also eager to tell them stories about the Virgin Mary, who plays such an important part in the childhood of European Catholics, but here he ran into an unexpected obstacle. It turned out that the warm place which the Virgin might have found in the hearts of the pygmies was already occupied by Queen Elizabeth II.

The Queen of England looms large in the political aware-ness of the natives in the more accessible parts of New Guinea, just as the person of Queen Victoria must have loomed throughout the whole of the British Empire. The average Australian patrol officer, struggling to explain the structure of authority to a village of illiterate natives, finds that he can conjure up little enthusiasm for a stranger in Port Moresby who goes by the title of Administrator, Papua/New Guinea. So he goes straight to the romantic head of the pyramid, a mysterious woman countless miles away across the ocean who is beautiful beyond imagination and powerful past belief, but is usually most benevolent to those who behave themselves. In the pidgin English which is the *lingua franca* of the territory, the familiar title of this impressive lady is Big Fella Number One Missus. How could the Virgin Mary compete?

The most powerful concepts of mankind, whether *bakhshish* or Coca-Cola, seem able to creep into inaccessible places ahead of any known contact. Even the pygmies, in their almost impenetrable jungle, had heard of the Queen. Indeed, a mutual admiration for her father had been at first the only real contact between Manning and O'Halloran and their hosts, until the mere repetition of his name became a talisman of friendship. About ten years later, the pygmies suddenly began to chatter with excitement about this new Big Fella Number One Missus, word of whom came from someone who had met someone who far away in the jungle had met someone who had met someone. Thus, some five years after the event, news reached the two white men that George VI had died. They held a simple memorial service.

The pygmies' knowledge of pidgin English had originally extended very little beyond the title of His Majesty, but over the years Manning and O'Halloran had taught them the rudiments of the language – largely by repeating the names of basic objects until even the parrot might have picked them up. (The grammatical structure of pidgin English is delightfully uncomplicated; the minimum nouns and verbs necessary to the concept are laid out in line, and are then mortared loosely together with the ubiquitous word 'along', which stands in for almost every conjunction or preposition.) The two Europeans had been less successful in mastering the language of their hosts. The pygmy idea of teaching was to launch straight into rapid conversation. With the pupils' first stumbling attempts to isolate and repeat a particular phrase, the teachers had invariably become speechless with giggles. Even now, twenty years later, J.K. acted as interpreter on any complicated matter. Otherwise the Europeans conversed with the pygmies in pidgin. And pidgin was the language of the scripture lessons.

Fortunately the Queen's sex had left a major title vacant for Christ. He became known to all the class, in spite of considerable opposition from the priest, as Big Fella Number One Mista. And it was inevitable that the similarity of the two titles should link the pair more closely in the minds of the pygmies than would be allowed by their more orthodox devotees.

'Father me like along savee,' began someone in the front row in a loud but almost indecipherable mumble. The surrealist effect of the whole scene was heightened when any of the twenty-five warriors decided to ask a question, because Murgatreud had again left no mouth-hole in the helmets and it was as hard to decide who was speaking as to interpret his words.

'Now hold it a minute, me old friend, let's see who you are,' said O'Halloran, and then translated himself into the jargon. 'Me no see voice along who.'

A hand near the centre of the curving row of knights was raised. The warrior, indistinguishable from the others except by his arms and legs, was sitting only two away from the elegant arabesques which concealed Chief Alalo, so the question probably came, O'Halloran reasoned, from one of the old man's sons.

'Right then,' he said.

The shout mumbled out from the eyes of the helmet once again. 'Father me like along savee Big Fella Number One Mista he sing-sing along Big Fella Number One Missus along night?'

'What?' said O'Halloran, startled.

'Big Fella Number One Mista he sing-sing along Big Fella Number One Missus along night?'

'Big Fella Number One Mista he *sing* along Number One Missus along night?' repeated O'Halloran slowly, and, it must have seemed to the pygmies, a trifle idiotically. 'Now why on earth should he want to do that, why on earth should he sing along ... ?'

But the questioner was now holding up his two index fingers, side by side, and rubbing the edges of them together. And there was a sound of metallic drumming along the front row as the warriors leaned backwards and forwards, thumping their fists against their breastplates, much as diners at a banquet might formally thump the table to salute a particularly good joke in an after-dinner speech. It was plain that the harmony imagined between Christ and the Queen was more than vocal.

O'Halloran was quite flustered. 'Certainly not,' he hastened to add, 'certainly not indeed. He never has and He never will. Now get this into your tiny heads. Big Fella Number One Mista He along one place along one time, Big Fella Number One Missus she along another place along another time two thousand years, that'll be . . .' but in his confusion he couldn't calculate the number of moons, which were the units of pygmy chronology. 'Quite different altogether,' he ended lamely, 'the very idea.'

But the pygmies were also interested in aspects of Christ more acceptable to the missionary. It was possible to arouse their amazement at some, but not all, of the miracles. If He could raise bodies from the dead, they had expected no less; that five small loaves and two fishes should be enough for five thousand did not greatly impress them; but they were astounded that He had been able to walk on the water.

'He walk along water along river he soon along sea,' observed someone. Much of pygmy mythology was concerned with where the tumultuous river went to, and the lessons in pidgin English had provided this place with the name sea – though it did less than justice to the watery Valhalla of their dreams.

'He walks along sea all along time,' O'Halloran had replied, thinking only of Galilee. And the pygmies had fallen into a respectful silence, lost in awe at the thought of a man who could walk on the waters of the sea they had in mind.

The crucifixion always sent an excited shudder through the group. The brass crucifix was detached from its pole and passed from hand to hand. With the interest of the primitive mind in small particulars, they wanted to know every aspect of the problem. How exactly was the cross made? How were the poles held together? How was Christ got up there, and once up there how held in position? O'Halloran had never asked himself such questions, but he had once seen a performance of the York mystery plays which include, in their crucifixion scene, precisely this sort of detail. From his memories of that afternoon he was able to make various suggestions which seemed to satisfy his listeners.

The Second Coming struck, at first, no response at all. But when O'Halloran, very properly extending the indiscriminate embrace of the Christian faith to its latest adherents, emphasized that the Second Coming was just as likely to occur among themselves as among any other believers, and any day too, their response was immediate. They took the news intensely personally, in a way which thrilled O'Halloran. It meant that at last his words were reaching the heart.

'Big Fella Number One Mista come again along me along Alalo?' asked Alalo.

O'Halloran nodded. 'Could be. Could well be. Come again along Alalo.'

Someone else asked the same question, and then someone else. 'Come again along me?' 'Come again along me?' It was turning into a game, but a truly educational game, a game of spiritual involvement, a game which O'Halloran encouraged. Everyone had to ask the question, even lesser members of the tribe behind the gleaming front row, even women, even children. 'Come again along me?' 'Come again along me?' Hands were shooting up all round, people were jumping up and down to catch the priest's attention. He nodded, nodded happily, continued to nod. 'Could be, could well be, come again along you all, God bless you all,' he said.

But the front row, the twenty-five warriors, felt it was time to reassert themselves. The game behind had gone far enough. A hand shot up from one gleaming suit of armour, a hand which had already been accorded a place at the Second Coming, and the group fell silent to make way for the loud muffled question from the helmet.

'Big Fella Number One Mista He black fella?'

'Good Lord, no,' answered O'Halloran with a laugh. The very most he would allow Him was an unusually heavy sun-tan, the result of the climate in the Middle East and of an outdoor life, but this subtlety of refinement was beyond expression in pidgin English. As it turned out, the nearest

6

approximation that could be achieved was 'Big Fella Number One Mista He white fella'. But the information seemed perfectly acceptable to the crowd.

After this, further physical details were needed – understandable among a people who now expected any day the Second Coming in their midst. As regards height, O'Halloran was forced to be fairly specific. Knowing the pygmies' admiration of size, their own most conspicuous lack, he felt it improper that Christ should be shorter than anyone present. So He was announced to be a fraction larger than Dr Manning – stooping, admittedly, anything else would have been a most improbable exaggeration – but this nevertheless established Him at well over six feet. For the other characteristics, a more generalized impression could be given, and O'Halloran fell back on the post-Pre-Raphaelite watercolours which had illustrated the family Bibles of his youth. So the Person the pygmies heard about was an elegant blond hippy, in tasteful hessian robes, strolling through a landscape which most nearly approximated to St Ives with camels.

At last the curiosity of the company was sated, and the warriors in the front row became impatient for the martial exercises which were to follow. O'Halloran wound up the proceedings with a short prayer which the tribe had learnt phonetically and could now recite with him. It had been a most encouraging session.

The military part of the morning always began with a solemn march, to the accompaniment of one of those fighting Anglican hymns which *Ancient and Modern* describes as Processional. These were provided from the school memories of Manning rather than O'Halloran, for they had long ago agreed not to indulge in sectarian rivalries as to what precise aspect of Christianity was made available to the pygmies. The battle of the missionaries, all too familiar between ambitious soul-totting priests in other primitive territories, was not to be allowed to intrude into the private and remote glade of this pair of friends. Whatever part of Christianity most appealed to the pygmy mind should be theirs for the asking, and hymns ranked high.

74

Murgatreud's own traditions of worship would have been welcome too, if they had proved suitable. But he had been born a Lutheran, had become a Mormon when involved in some delicate but lucrative transactions of a personal nature in Salt Lake City, had embraced the Jewish faith in order to collect over the years a series of top-secret packages in Israel, had successfully passed as a Muslim, after memorizing sufficient snippets of the Koran to meet most contingencies, when delivering the same series of packages to their destination in Saudi Arabia, and was at the moment officially a Zoroastrian so as to facilitate a long-term contract with a rich Parsee of Bombay. It was decided that he was best left out of account in the matter of the pygmies' faith.

The favourite hymns were 'Onward, Christian Soldiers', 'Fight the Good Fight with All Thy Might', and 'Stand up, Stand up for Jesus, Ye Soldiers of the Cross'. After the warriors had buckled their cuishes on to their thighs and their greaves on their shins, had bridged the gap between the two with a knee cop and had rounded off by fixing a solleret over the top of the foot, they would form up into a squad, four abreast and six deep, with Chief Alalo out in front. Their swords rested on their right shoulders, where a yokel props his scythe. Then, with the muffled words of one of the hymns buzzing from their helmets, they would begin their solemn march across the clearing. The tunes, so brisk and cheerful in the school chapels of England, were taken here much like a dirge. Murgatreud's suits of armour did not make for a brisk pace. It was hard to bend either hip or knee, and the weight was considerable. The twenty-five men moved forward with the jerky mechanical movements of the toy astronaut who had so profitably failed to impress Chief Alalo.

When they reached the far end of the clearing, they turned and spread out. Meanwhile, all the other men of the tribe had lined up opposite them. Yelling war cries, they now advanced, with bows and arrows at the ready, towards the armoured men. This was the high point of the morning. Here a traditional pygmy battle was enacted, and here the magic of the new weapons was each day fully revealed. (Manning had explained to Murgatreud that on the rare occasions when two tribes engaged in an organized set-to, the custom was for them to fire a single volley of arrows at each other from opposite sides of a clearing. They would then move closer and repeat the process with spears. After this second volley, the tribe with more men standing would chase their rivals unceremoniously from the field. Clearly, Alalo, rejecting the best of Hamley's for an improvised tin can, had recognized the advantages of armour in such an encounter.)

Each morning the naked pygmies continued to advance until they were within easy bow-shot of Chief Alalo's line. Then, with whoops of excitement, they released their arrows. The warriors had by now closed the eye-holes in their helmets (a small visor could be pulled down from above, as if lowering sun-glasses from forehead to nose), and like blind gods they stared up at the sky, from which the shafts would fall. They seemed to bask in them, moving their blank and upturned faces slowly from side to side, as one might in a shower of warm rain. And they were right to be confident. Murgatreud had designed the suits of armour for just this situation. From the front the entire body, from fingernail to toe, was shielded by metal, and it was the prudent overlapping of the plates which made movement so difficult. The arrows clattered harmlessly down with the sound of hail on a tin roof. And when the last had been deflected, and silence had returned, these men of steel would open their grey eyes and advance slowly back across the clearing.

They were in line abreast, and they waved their swords before them as if to reap a harvest of bodies. Now the war cries of their naked enemies were turned to exaggerated screams of terror, equally enjoyable to perform in the circumstances. Backwards and forwards scurried the panic-stricken mimes. They flung themselves on the ground in positions of supplication, they offered their bows as a bargain, they wept and tore their hair, all to no avail. The knights of the red cross came on inexorably. A few brave spirits, spotting a gap in the line, nipped through at the risk of a slash, but most of the tribe continued to retreat. When there was no more space left, they shinned and swung up jungle trees at the edge of the clearing for their final refuge, still shrieking their dismay. And at last the relentless knights stopped, removed the helmets, and, smiling with undisguised pleasure, awaited congratulation. For all concerned it was a most satisfactory pageant.

The remainder of the military proceedings was taken up with single combat between armed men, in the local tradition of bash-swopping, blow for blow, clang by clang, which had originally given Dong and Ding their names. The idea of sword-play had not yet occurred to the pygmies, and Murgatreud was in no hurry to suggest it.

Then followed the medical lesson and the turn of Dr Manning. It became customary for one of those engaged in single combat to fall and pretend to be wounded. Four pygmies would hurry from the edge of the clearing with a stretcher of bamboo poles and woven vine. On to it they would bundle the man of metal, and then stagger back with him, gawky and inflexible as a lobster, to the safety of the trees. There his armour would be removed without any co-operation on his part – a matter requiring considerable practice – and Manning would create somewhere on his anatomy, with red dye, a particularly gory wound. This would be lovingly washed clean by the pygmies, daubed with iodine, then dressed and bound with new crepe bandages from the medicine chest provided by Murgatreud. One day Manning demonstrated the principle of the tourniquet, but the pygmies responded with such alarming zest, each being determined to take a turn with the tightening, that he decided to postpone that lesson. But he did score a considerable success with the kiss of life, and soon everyone was proficient at administering it. It was only later discovered that this useful piece of first-aid had radically altered the sexual habits of the tribe. Until then their love-play had been restricted to a rhythmic rolling of forehead against forehead.

There was one genuine medical crisis. A few of the warriors had taken to leaving their eye-guards open under the storm of arrows – it added to their excitement to see what they were surviving – and one day an arrow did go into a man's eye. The edge of the helmet deflected it slightly and it lodged between the bone of the eye-socket and outer edge of the eye. The first problem was to remove the helmet, which involved cutting very slowly through the shaft of the arrow in an area of operation limited by the opening of the metal eye-hole. When this had been achieved, the extraction of the barb itself required a full-scale operation. The patient was placed on a pair of tables in front of the white men's huts, and all the resources of the new medicine chest were required – anaesthetic, sterilizing agents, forceps, clips, ligatures and a more delicate scalpel than anything in Manning's old Vaselined set. The operation took an hour, and not only was the man's life saved – unthinkable after such a wound under previous circumstances – but three months later he was beginning to recover partial vision in that eye. As he worked on the operation, and later paid regular visits to his patient, Manning felt an old professional pride begin to stir in him, something he had not known for more than twenty years. Wasn't this, after all, why he had come to these godforsaken parts?

So the mornings of study and practice in the village clearing were as much a time of discovery and excitement for O'Halloran and Manning as for the pygmy tribe. In the early days Murgatreud was always there too, directing the squad in the use of armour. But soon, once they had the hang of it, he began to attend less regularly. He and Dong and Ding could be heard working away behind locked doors in their high-walled smithy. Making, presumably, yet more suits of armour for the tribe. Or further refinements.

XVII

Murgatreud took the seventh and last slice of tinned pineapple and passed the bowl with the remaining juice towards O'Halloran. Another large consignment of goods had been parachuted in, mainly a new supply of sheets of metal, but also some added comforts around the camp. Pineapple slices were another of Murgatreud's specialties, preferably with a crystallized cherry nestling in the middle of each. They reminded him of the girls in Hawaii.

'Do you not think,' mused O'Halloran tentatively, as he spooned what was left of the juice into his bowl, 'do you not think that sooner or later with all these martial exercises the little fellows will want to go and bash somebody? Do you not think that? Maybe?'

'Ya gotta point,' said Murgatreud, 'no kiddin, sacrebleu, ya gotta point,' and he downed the last morsel of pineapple as though that concluded the conversation.

After a pause Manning, as usual, stepped in. 'I think our good friend here is implying, is this the sort of thing we should encourage? What are we here for if we let them carry on in their own barbaric ways?'

'Hot ferdomma, da schmucks is crusaders. So crusade.'

'That was not maybe quite the crusade we had in mind,' ventured O'Halloran.

'Onward, Christian Soldiers,' sang Murgatreud thumping the table for emphasis on each beat.

'Usually taken as a metaphor,' said Manning.

'Nix by me.'

'Marching *as* to war,' emphasized O'Halloran. But it turned out that Murgatreud's thoughts were anyway running along the same lines. Nothing would be gained, he readily agreed, if Chief Alalo and his men merely entered the nearest village and beat up the inhabitants. Anyway – and he seemed to regard this practical detail as clinching the matter – wearing all that armour they would never be able to catch anyone to beat up. But what an effective advertisement for the recent birth of civilization in this tiny valley, what a demonstration of the irresistible strength of Christianity and the white man's way, if Alalo and his armour-plated platoon marched into the centre of a rival village – something which they would only be able to do thanks to their new weapons – and then, instead of the usual heathen massacre and brutality, left some gentle symbol of friendship, a token of peace and goodwill towards men!

'Such as what, maybe?'

'Hot ferdomma, Father, me, Murgatreud, miserable sinner, nowya ask?'

'Well?' insisted Manning.

'Cross, natch. Mamma mia, what else?'

The priest and the doctor had to concede the force of the argument. It would indeed, in the complete absence of any violence, be most effective. And so it was decided that Chief Alalo and his men should bear with them, as a banner, a large wooden cross entirely covered with fresh jungle flowers, and that they should erect this symbol of love in the centre of the neighbouring village and then return. And it was further agreed that the raid – they laughed at the misnomer – should take place without delay.

O'Halloran was given the task of persuading Chief Alalo to carry out this plan. And such, apparently, was the power of the cross on the armour, and the desire of the pygmies to fall in with whatever the magic of the new symbol demanded, that the old man readily agreed.

XVIII

The nearest village was the one over the hill, where the first parachute drop had fallen. It was out of the question for the forces to march that far in their full paraphernalia, so the plan was for the rest of the tribe to carry the various items of armour through the narrow jungle paths, along which the twenty-five athletes would stroll unencumbered. Near the enemy village they would be quietly dressed and then, bearing aloft the flower-bedecked cross, they would march into the village singing 'Onward, Christian Soldiers'. Once in the centre of the village – all opposition would melt away after the first flight of arrows had proved ineffectual – they were to set up the cross and sing the first verse of 'God Save the Queen' (here, and here alone, for the sake of the rhythm the pygmies were prepared to forgo the full title of Big Fella Number One Missus). This done, they would withdraw to where the rest of the tribe awaited them, disrobe, and make their way back through the jungle to the village. Both size and clumsiness prevented the three white men from accompanying the expedition. But J.K. was to go with it and bring back a report.

The troops set off in high spirits. Chief Alalo shook hands with Murgatreud, Manning and O'Halloran and then slipped into the dense undergrowth, followed by his team of twenty-four picked men. Behind them came J.K. with the cross of flowers, and after him a long string of bearers with bundles of armour on their heads.

'Pray God it may go as planned,' said O'Halloran.

'Amen,' said Manning.

'Smile,' said Murgatreud. 'Itsa cinch.'

To while away the time, Manning and O'Halloran played six-pack bezique, one of the amusements included by the Contact in the latest consignment. They were like two nervous schoolmasters waiting for news of an away match.

Murgatreud was unable to join them. As always these days, he was too busy with the pressure of work in the smithy.

Four hours later the tribe was back, jubilant. They brought with them a few skulls – old ones, very old, they hastened to assure the white men – and they insisted that all had gone peacefully, according to plan.

And J.K. confirmed this. In the privacy of the white men's clearing at the top of the village, after serving them with Cinzano and unsalted cashews, he gave a full account of the expedition.

'It really did turn out to be an awfully good show,' he began, 'absolutely wizard.'

'I wish you wouldn't use that phrase,' said Manning.

'Well, you did.'

'Once. To my infinite regret. Go on.'

'Well, we kitted them up only a couple of hundred yards from the other village, and off they went. Chief Alalo carried the cross.'

Here J.K. mimed the stiff marching gait of a fully armed man, and provided his own accompaniment.

> 'Onward, Christian soldiers,
>   Marching as to war,
> With the cross of Jesus
>   Going on before,

and it jolly well was going on before, at a hell of a lick, too.'

'J.K., your language.'

'Sorry, Father. But old Alalo was right out in front, and by now they'd been seen, and out they all came, screaming and yelling their little heads off, and they'd got their bows, and our boys stopped and closed their eyes, and then the arrows came. Nothing. And it suddenly went quiet. Very quiet. They just stared. They couldn't believe it. Then Alalo went on again,

> "Like a mighty army,
>   Moves the Church of God,"

et cetera, et cetera,' and all this J.K. briefly enacted, 'and then they came dashing forward with their spears and hurled those. Again nothing. Again they just stood and stared, you would have laughed. And suddenly they turned and ran, and by the time Alalo was in the middle of the village there was no one left, place was empty, and then we came up, and we helped them put up the cross, and we all stood there and sang

> "God save our gracious queen,
> Long live our noble queen,"'

and here J.K. stood to attention, 'right to the last line, and then we came away.' And that, as far as J.K. was concerned, was the end of the story.

'And what about the skulls?' prompted Manning.

'What skulls?'

'There were skulls brought back,' said O'Halloran.

'Oh, those. Just a few old skulls that were lying about.'

'From the rafters?'

'Ancestors?'

'You were in their huts?'

J.K. shrugged and looked embarrassed. 'Maybe one or two,' he said. But Murgatreud came to his rescue.

'See it my way,' he said, 'so wotsa skulla two between friends, huh?' And there it was left.

XIX

The next two weeks were quiet. The crusaders were proud of themselves, resting on their laurels. Manning and O'Halloran decided to overlook the matter of the skulls. Murgatreud was little in evidence. He and Dong and Ding were almost permanently away from the village. They were out in the jungle, it seemed, looking for certain types of wood that they needed for new projects. The morning lessons in divinity, warfare and medicine continued as before.

But one day, when O'Halloran was leading up to the marriage at Cana, and Manning was sitting near by arranging his materials for a demonstration of the splint, there was a rude interruption. From the edge of the jungle up towards the top of the clearing there emerged a group of small men in gleaming armour. For one moment it seemed an incomprehensible apparition. The warriors in the front row of the class glanced at each other in case any of their number had played truant. Meanwhile the men in armour had spread themselves out into a line, just as in the exercise which followed divinity. In front of them stood a man holding a wooden cross decorated with wild flowers. Still it was like a mirror image, a double vision, a *déjà vu*. But now the line was moving stiffly down the clearing, and the crosses on their breast-plates and helmets were blue, and from their eye-holes came the sounds of a hymn, muffled and inaccurate but still just recognizable to Manning and O'Halloran from the sturdy self-confidence of Luther's own magnificent tune:

'Ein' feste Burg ist unser Gott,
Ein' gute Wehr und Waffen.'

By now everyone had realized that this was an enemy. The tribe knew enough about armour not to waste time sending off a volley of arrows, but there was chaos as warriors scrabbled for greaves and cuishes and struggled in the turmoil to strap them on. No one had succeeded in fully arming himself before the line of intruders reached the class. The only hope was to scurry for the safety of the jungle, away from the flailing line of swords. Clutching a miscellaneous assortment of pieces of armour, Alalo's pygmies scattered. One or two tripped and narrowly missed a slash. Several vital sections of armour were deserted in the rush. Even Manning and O'Halloran had to make a quick getaway.

'Look here, what on earth is this? You have no right to be here,' Manning had complained indignantly, and pointlessly, to the advancing line of metal-clad strangers. 'The peace of God be upon you, and go your way in peace,' O'Halloran had conjured them, holding out his crucifix in their direction, face to face as it were with the flowery cross, but to no avail. The two Europeans, unwilling to risk a dash through the line, were forced for the first time in their lives to melt into the jungle.

The line wheeled, once the open ground was empty, and converged on the huts of the village, grouped under large trees beside the clearing. An old woman emerged from one as the invaders reached it. Immediately in front of her was the man with the cross of flowers. He brought it down with a crack on her skull, and she fell among a scattered posy. (This incident later raised some doubts as to how Alalo's men had established the cross in the neighbouring village two weeks before.) The knights then ransacked the houses, retrieving their own captured skulls and taking a few more besides.

Some of Alalo's warriors were beginning to appear, tentative but fully armed, round the edge of the clearing. Manning and O'Halloran made a very hurried crossing to the enclave at the top. They found Murgatreud with Dong and Ding in his smithy.

'What the hell is going on, if you'll pardon the expression?' said O'Halloran.

'Whether you'll pardon it or not, what the hell is going on?' added Manning.

'Coolit amigos,' said Murgatreud, handing a red-hot section of armour in a pair of tongs to Dong, 'so wassamatta?'

'The matter!' spluttered O'Halloran.

'Thumpa guy'll thumpya back,' said Murgatreud with a shrug, adding, 'Saylavee.' But at this moment a half-armoured Alalo came panting into the compound.

'All tribe no like along Alalo tribe fight along armour,' he gasped, in what seemed a combination of statement, query and accusation.

Murgatreud handed him a ready-prepared bundle of about

a dozen bamboo spears, each at least a yard longer than the usual pygmy version and every one with a cruel metal point on the end.

'Poke along enemy poke along eye,' he explained to the old man, prodding towards the open eye-holes in Alalo's helmet. 'Enemy close along eye push along enemy fall along down,' he continued, and he came up to Alalo and gave him a shove on the breastplate. 'So move,' said Murgatreud, turning the old chief to propel him out of the compound.

Alalo's men were all now in full armour, and they quickly grasped the advantage offered by the spears. With one of these a man could advance towards an enemy knight and jab at the eye-holes in his helmet, while still safely out of reach of the slashing sword. His rival would soon, in self-defence, lower his eye-guard and stand there blinded. The assailant then had only to lumber closer, and a shove with both hands would be sufficient to topple the heavily weighted man backwards to the ground. Soon at least six of the invaders were flat on their backs and the rest had made a hasty retreat.

With the six on the ground there was a temporary stalemate. Alalo's men in their own full armour were unable to stoop sufficiently to force a blade between the joints of a fallen knight's mail, or to roll him over so as to expose his less well-protected back. They were reduced to belabouring their victims ineffectually with swords, like a child beating a tortoise. But soon unarmed pygmies ventured forth to lend a hand. They were heaving the unfortunate captives over on to their bellies when Manning and O'Halloran intervened. To the great regret of the tribe, the Europeans insisted on a truce, sweetening the loss with the six enemy suits of armour which were kept as battle trophies while their naked occupants, pathetic sweaty little creatures quivering with fear, were sent with a farewell bouquet of kicks stumbling back into the jungle.

XX

Chief Alalo's anger at an evident betrayal of trust was neatly turned by Murgatreud. Within half an hour of the battle the old man was back in the compound, as indignant as before but by now more collected. Why had Murgatreud betrayed him by selling armour to his enemies?

Murgatreud looked surprised and slightly pained. Betrayed? ('Go along stop go along', in pidgin English.) Had he not provided the chief with twelve magnificent metal-headed spears, entirely new and magical weapons? Moreover, at the moment of crisis, had he not handed them over without so much as a pause to discuss the price, on a basis of pure trust? And had these splendid weapons not won a crushing victory? And had that victory not resulted in the capture of six valuable suits of armour, entirely free?

With all this Alalo could only agree. Murgatreud, it now transpired, had been intending to charge a very low price for the spears – only fifteen small gold ornaments or three large ones. This was actually less than the value of those six new suits of armour, on which Murgatreud would be happy to change the colour of the crosses for nothing. So, looked at another way, Alalo was in fact getting the dozen spears entirely free.

It was less than half an hour before Alalo had fully grasped the force of this argument, and the time would have been shorter but for the vagaries of pidgin English. The old man went away, as grateful as ever, with a promise to deliver the golden images before nightfall.

The renewed opposition of Manning and O'Halloran was more serious, but no mention was made of it until dinner that evening. O'Halloran, as a gesture, was in his old cassock, ending in tatters around his chins. Manning was slightly ashamed to be wearing the new dinner-jacket, which had arrived for him in the latest consignment, but, frankly, by now the old one looked ridiculous. It was he who broached the subject.

'You know, old chap, this sort of thing isn't on. The thing must be said, it really isn't.'

Murgatreud looked amazed and said nothing. He filled the awkward gap with a well-laden fork of steak-and-kidney pudding.

'I mean, I'm talking about this afternoon. I mean, for example, where did those little fellows get their suits of armour?'

Murgatreud tapped his own chest, chewing.

'Obviously. Of course. Where else?' agreed Manning.

Murgatreud was happy to concede in silence that there was no answer to that question. O'Halloran took up the case. His manner was more openly indignant than Manning's.

'It's a scandal, that's what it is, a scandal in the eyes of the Lord. And blasphemy too. Yes, blasphemy. Down from the trees they came, wearing the holy sign of the cross and singing a hymn . . .'

'Insisted,' Murgatreud interrupted, through a full mouth, 'little schmucks insisted. Magic song for armour like Alalo.'

' . . . I don't care what they insisted, it was you taught them a Christian hymn and gave the holy cross to a bunch of ignorant savages who don't know so much about Christianity as Hail Mary or How's your Father . . .'

'Are you sure that's a Christian . . .' began Manning in evident surprise, but the priest was not to be deflected.

' . . . don't know the first thing about the Christian faith, plain ignorant heathens, that's all they are, it's a scandal . . .'

'Scandal?' Murgatreud at last seemed ready to take a proper part in the conversation. He ferreted out the remaining morsels in his cheeks, swallowed, and slowly dabbed his napkin round his mouth with a special almost obscene attention to both corners, where the pink tip of his tongue had prepared the way. 'Scandal now? Scandal fa who? Blunt, ja? Frank, ja?' he said, as if asking permission.

They nodded. Of course. Among men. Why not?

Murgatreud stubbed a pudgy forefinger at the two of them

before he spoke. 'Heathen savages halfmile mission twenty year dunno nix truefaith, notta word. Scandal fa who? Mission wallah sit 'n a bum twenty year 'n do nuttin, some kinda dumb scheisskopf, na? Scandal fa who? Blunt 'n frank. Na?'

It was more blunt than they had expected, more frank than they were accustomed to, but the point struck home. It was an area in which they felt particularly vulnerable. Without a fight they allowed the subject to be changed. They began to apologize, to explain. Wearily, as if fragile with ill-health, they outlined their special problems, the difficulty of communication, the lack of supplies, the special friendship offered them by this one tribe which had somehow estranged them from the others . . .

Murgatreud cut them short. 'Ja so, 'n finito.' But things were different now. Already another tribe was eager for their services, for the magic of their medicine and their faith, another tribe as talented as Alalo's. He plunged into the strong-room adjoining his hut and brought out some of the golden artefacts with which the neighbouring tribe of blue-cross knights had so recently presented him.

They were passed gently from hand to hand. In a subdued way they were extraordinarily beautiful – simple abstract shapes in gold, exquisitely fashioned and perforated with holes to give a lace-like effect.

'Notsa savage, huh?'

'They're beautiful.'

'Quite beautiful.' Secretly the priest found them preferable to Alalo's images because they were non-phallic (though later, when this particular tribe required more sophisticated weapons, it was discovered that they too had in reserve some spectacular phallic creations).

'World should see, huh?' said Murgatreud, and he went on to ask why they had felt Alalo's artefacts deserved a showing in the West if these did not. How could they, people in their position, take a partisan attitude? Did they intend to turn a blind eye and a deaf ear to the countless tribes who would soon be clamouring for their help and guidance? If so, what was their mission? Why were they here?

Once again, and once again to their own surprise, the priest and the doctor found it hard to deny the fat man his arguments. Out came the *marrons glacés*. Out came the Napoleon brandy. There were three bulbous glasses now, and even some to spare. In silence, alarmed perhaps by the upheaval that was to be thrust upon them in their gentle way of life, each of the two missionaries stared down into the glass orb where the brandy chased round and round. Murgatreud broke the stillness. But gently.

'Albert Schweitzer, say, man like him dooalotta good?'

'Oh, very much so.'

'Yes, indeed.'

Murgatreud topped up their glasses. There was another long pause.

'David Livingstone,' said Manning.

'Saint Francis Xavier,' offered O'Halloran.

'Winfrid or Boniface,' continued Manning.

'Winfrid *and* Boniface,' suggested Murgatreud, expansively. 'Why not?'

'Same chap. Different names. You know the way, in those days.'

Murgatreud offered the brandy again – too soon, as it turned out, but the gesture was appreciated.

'The Blessed Raymond Lull. Saint René Goupil, who fell to an Iroquois tomahawk when making the sign of the cross over a child.' O'Halloran was beginning to enjoy himself. 'Holy Martyrs all.'

'Florence Nightingale,' said the doctor.

'Saint Felipe de Jesus de la Casas. The Blessed Rudolf Acquaviva.'

'Ziegenbalg, Plütschau and Schwartz.'

Murgatreud perked up. 'No kiddin?'

'First Protestant mission,' Manning explained. 'On the Coromandel coast.'

'The Blessed Bishop Gabriel Dufresse, beheaded in Sezuan. John of Monte Corvino. The Blessed Ignacio Delgado.'

Quietly the other two removed O'Halloran's brandy glass, and shared its contents between their own.

'The Blessed Berard of Carbio. Martyrs all. Dead every one. Saint Joseph Mukasa. Saint Antoine Daniel.'

Manning and Murgatreud caught each other's eye and smiled. And yet the mere recital of O'Halloran's predecessors had a pleasantly uplifting effect, regardless of their particular fates. The three friends – the classic trio of priest, doctor and merchant – went to bed, that night, united as never before.

XXI

The system spread as rapidly as Murgatreud had predicted. The neighbouring tribe, after their one brief discomfiture, realized that it was better policy to attack those who were still unarmed rather than their own equals. The six missing suits of armour were replaced at a very reasonable price by Murgatreud, and soon a full complement of knights, resplendent once again in their blue crosses, was able to make a series of successful raids on other near-by villages. Each of these villages then sent a delegation to knock at the private jungle door into the smithy, where they negotiated for a consignment of suits of armour. These in turn now attacked the slightly more peripheral tribes, which were still unarmed, and so the circle grew.

Soon the original tribes at the centre discovered that all their immediate neighbours were armed, and they too needed to return to the smithy for the latest sophistication which would give them once more a temporary edge. Thus each successive wave of armaments spread like a ripple from the centre. Murgatreud stoutly maintained that the only proper code for an arms supplier was the high principle of absolute impartiality. No one was refused.

'Sure is a swell scheme,' the parrot would usually comment at some stage in the delicate negotiations between each group of pygmies and Murgatreud over the purchase of armour. 'Sure is,' it would invariably insist some seconds later, regardless of the terms.

The pygmies were much impressed by such oracular interventions, particularly after the bird's precise meaning had been explained. The phrase gradually became a conventional one throughout the territory, used almost indiscriminately to express any form of enthusiasm. 'Sure is a swell scheme,' one pygmy would say, in greeting, agreement, or congratulation, to another. 'Sure is,' the other would reply. It was, said O'Halloran, like 'Top o' the mornin'' to an Irishman.

To keep pace with the ever-growing demand, work at the smithy was continuous. Dong and Ding became supervisory foremen, and a dozen other members of Chief Alalo's tribe were trained to carry out the basic production routines under their guidance. Murgatreud himself, occupied now for much of the time in business sessions with his scores of rival clients, had to limit his labour in the smithy to the design and forging of prototypes.

The slow leap-frogging progress of the weaponry towards unattainable perfection followed the rough lines which Murgatreud had already discovered in *Der Waffenschmied* and the other books, but he now derived the details of his inspiration from one work in particular, *Die Kriegswaffen in ihren geschichtlichen Entwickelungen von den ältesten Zeiten bis auf die Gegenwart*, a magnificent compendium, characteristically Germanic in its thoroughness, which gave, for example, detailed drawings of more than two hundred different styles of helmet. Here he was able to discover the exact next stage required by his customers. The inherent weakness of the pygmies' first helmets – the large eye-hole which was so vulnerable to a spear-thrust unless completely sealed – was overcome by providing only a narrow slit to peer through (a style popular in Bavaria in the thirteenth century), the slit being too thin to admit an arrow or the first generation of pygmy spears. The next and complementary development was a spear with a broad but thin blade, much like those carried by the Zulus, which would neatly fit through the eye-slit. This was followed by helmets in which the entire front of the face was dotted with tiny holes, like the top of a pepper pot, Murgatreud's own adaptation of a helmet worn by Charles V at the conquest of Tunis in 1535. Each hole was too small for any dangerous missile to pass through it, and by constantly moving his head from side to side, like a Martian scanning the landscape, the pygmy knight inside was just able to build up a composite picture of what was in front of him and so carry on with the fighting.

With cutting and prodding thus effectively ruled out, the next stage was bashing and crushing. It is just as damaging to crush a helmet on to the occupant's skull as to cut through it, and Murgatreud was able to find in his manual a wide variety of weapons for this purpose. He began with simple clubs, deriving their force from their heads of solid metal. To these he later added spikes, and then separated the head from the shaft in the celebrated Holy Water Sprinkler, a spiked ball on the end of a chain which allows for greater momentum.

The only answer to this second generation of weapons was thicker armour – and so the business progressed. To describe each stage in detail would require an entire history of medieval warfare, through which Murgatreud now hurried his clients with almost indecent haste. He also added a few refinements from other sources. The primitive bolas, with its heavy stones whirling at the end of three or four thongs, was successful for a while in entangling advancing knights, and even the lasso had its moments, but both were hard to control from inside a suit of armour. More successful, among weapons outside the main stream, was a genuine medieval item, the Fangeisen, or Catchpole, popular in fifteenth-century Germany (and even used as late as 1691 by the Austrians at the siege of Mons). It looked like a rather harmless pitchfork, with blunt ends, but between the two prongs was a metal bar on a spring.

The weapon was lunged at a knight's helmet, where it narrowed for the neck, and when the two prongs had passed on either side the spring-flap closed behind. The indignant fellow, still slashing in ineffectual rage, could then be led home as safely as a ringed bull.

XXII

Murgatreud gently drifted the cross of the telescopic sight till it covered the cross on the breastplate of the armoured figure a hundred yards away down the village clearing. Then, almost lascivious in his slow enjoyment of the moment, he squeezed the machine-gun's trigger. The first bullet knocked the target to the ground; those which followed so close behind sent it spinning up again, high into the air. Murgatreud eased his index finger and lazily pursued the whirling metallic dervish with the round circle of his viewfinder. He had not felt this peculiar blend of relaxed exhilaration since an afternoon of leisurely sniping, some years ago, from the safety of a client's penthouse in the Congo. As the suit of armour seemed to pause at the height of its trajectory, Murgatreud's hairline cross was on it again. Once more he caught it fair and square. It was as if the floating figure had been galvanized in mid-air by a sudden electric shock. With arms and legs splayed at impossible angles, it flew, like some rag-doll Nureyev, a further thirty yards down the clearing. Murgatreud rose from his knees and allowed himself a sense of modest pleasure. It had felt as easy as reaching out a long, long finger to give the target a playful prod in the belly.

The two lines of pygmies down either side of the clearing, absolutely silent before the gunfire, were now buzzing with excitement. But no one moved. No one was to move until after the third gun had spoken.

Murgatreud had lately become very defence-conscious. As he liked to point out, almost the entire treasure of the surrounding district was gathered into these few square yards, with only three friendless strangers to guard it against tens of thousands of bloodthirsty savages equipped with a very wide range of offensive weapons. So a wall ten feet high now surrounded the compound, consisting of a double layer of sturdy bamboo. At intervals of fifty yards, small bastions jutted out to give an unobstructed field of fire in all directions. For the same reason – the all-important field of fire – the jungle had been cut back to leave an open space on all sides of the fort, as the compound, in keeping with its new appearance, was now known. Even the side where the jungle used to reach to the very door of the smithy was cleared. No longer could clients arrive inconspicuously to negotiate with Murgatreud. But then no longer, now that he was firmly established as an equal friend to everyone, was it necessary that they should.

Three bastions faced down the clearing of Alalo's village, and today there was a machine-gun in each. They were intended, in case of emergency, to be used by the three white men, but although Murgatreud had coaxed Manning and O'Halloran into paying some slight attention to such necessary matters as the naming of parts, dismantling and assembly, loading, aim, and routine maintenance, nothing would persuade them to help him demonstrate the contraptions in front of the assembled pygmies.

Murgatreud rose from his knees and moved along the bamboo walkway which ran four feet below the top of the wall. In the central bastion the second gun awaited him. Again the armour leapt and spun, and the dummy knight spewed entrails of grass and leaves which, like the feathers of a shot bird, floated down to the ground long after the armour itself. By the time Murgatreud and the third gun had finished the work, the suit of armour was hardly solid enough to shuffle the passage of a bullet. Given the signal, the pygmies swarmed round to inspect the damage. That night at dinner it was agreed that one demonstration would prove sufficient.

For the more distant tribes, who might be beyond even the report of the machine-guns' powers, Murgatreud had another almost equally effective routine. He now carried in a holster on his hip a revolver, a more powerful weapon than the small automatic from his aeroplane, and after watching the traditional mock battle in far-away places he would sometimes stage a simple but impressive piece of showmanship. When the arrows had rained harmlessly down on the suits of armour, he would ask the local chief to remove his breastplate. This he would hang on a tree, and at point-blank range, carefully choosing a line at a right-angle to the metal, he would put a bullet through it just where the chief's heart had so recently been beating. Then, amid the general amazement and consternation, Dong and Ding would unwrap an identical breastplate, perhaps slightly more lavishly painted than the other, which Murgatreud would solemnly present to the grateful potentate.

'Sure is a swell scheme,' more often than not the chief would insist.

'Sure is,' agreed Dong and Ding and Murgatreud.

XXIII

It was most irritating. The collapsible altar, altar-rail, font and lectern had come in four large flat cardboard boxes, from the same firm in Rome as packed the holy wafers so tastefully that they looked like expensive chocolates, and the instructions emphasized that the kits were of a type to be easily and rapidly assembled. But O'Halloran had already struggled for hours with a perplexing variety of lengths of metal (a very light airmail alloy masquerading quite effectively as brass), and now finally he had had to move with all his scattered components from the interior of the church to less hallowed ground – for fear of a profanity creeping through his pursed and quivering lips, which held in readiness three different sizes of bolt.

His mistake, a result of his very natural excitement, had been to open all four boxes at once. Now, on the top of the pleasant knoll which had been uncovered behind the fort, the bewildered priest was making one last effort to lay his segments out flat on the grass in four groups vaguely suggestive of lectern, font, altar-rail and altar.

Behind him was his splendid new church, known already with some affection throughout the territory as 'the cathedral'. It was an elegant building, along much the same lines as the sacred house in the jungle, except that it had the addition of a steeple of tall bamboos at one end and neat Gothic windows set in the raffia mesh along both sides. The shapes of the windows had not been cut out, which would have weakened the fabric. Instead, the holes had been carefully drawn apart and stitched in position, allowing strands of warp and woof to wander across like lead in stained glass (a method known as drawn-thread work when used in silk), and sheets of polythene painted with scenes from the new illustrated Bibles were stretched across the inside. O'Halloran had been delighted to discover that the pictures in the Bibles, recently flown in by Murgatreud in bulk, were still in the style of his youth. Now his flock could see for themselves the gentle blond leader of Whom he brought word.

The mission, both religious and medical, had grown at an amazing pace. Each new tribe of Murgatreud's clients was eager for the services of the famous double medicine man, the pair of specialists who had divided between them what until now had always been one, the care of the spirit and the care of the flesh. For many weeks Manning and O'Halloran had set off each day on long trips through the jungle, often returning after dark. Later, as the distances increased, they needed to be away for several days. Like government officials on circuit, they would depart with a long train of bearers, on whose heads were the lightweight tents, the safari beds, the aluminium stove fuelled by small cylinders of butane gas, and all the other minor necessities provided by Murgatreud. Parachute drops were by now an almost daily event.

Finally, much to the secret relief of the priest and the doctor, the territory became so vast that their work had to be delegated. Manning had taught a group of young men from Alalo's tribe the basic necessities of first aid and now, with the tribe's original red cross adapted to its Swiss meaning, they travelled the outlying districts to pass on their skill. Another such group travelled on O'Halloran's behalf with the message of Rome, and a third gave instruction in pidgin English.

At home, Teresa had exchanged her schoolgirl's uniform for the robes of a convent novice. She and some other girls from Alalo's tribe, similarly clad, were known as the Tiny Sisters of Mercy. They assisted O'Halloran at Mass, an increasingly popular event in the week's calendar. And in the low, neat sick-bay, on the opposite side of the grassy knoll from the cathedral, Manning had taught four other girls the principles of nursing and the use of the new range of hospital equipment.

As a relief from the Meccano-like nightmare of altar and font, O'Halloran turned his attention to the smaller items of church furniture which had arrived in the same drop. These were more obliging. The four sides of an ornate gilt frame slotted together with gratifying ease to receive a canvas of the Virgin Mary, which seemed to have been painted by some subtle machine using the genuine materials. Putting the black tape round the passe-partout frames for the Stations of the Cross was time-consuming, but refreshingly simple. And the embroidered silk altar-cloth only needed unfolding.

Soothed, O'Halloran returned to his engineering, and an hour later it was done. All four items were complete. Only one small nut and a strange L-shaped object were left over. It was not until the next day that J.K. pointed out why the Bible kept sliding off the lectern and water dribbled out of the font. Each had borrowed a leg from the other.

XXIV

Manning lay back in the steaming tub, and controlled with a clutch of his toes the gentle flow of hot water. Noting with pleasure (a delightful mixture of pure research and pure relief) the moment at which the pain in his piles began to ease, he reached out for the thermometer and propped it near to vertical in his navel, which was a good three inches below the surface of the water. 95.2°, and last night it had been 95.1°. He was getting remarkably close to the optimum temperature in his new palliative treatment for the universal complaint, a treatment which as far as he knew was entirely his own discovery, being the precise opposite of the conventional cold rinse. After further observations he must certainly write up his findings for one of the journals.

Basking, as if the hot water were sunshine, he let his mind drift on among the problems of his larger project. He had undertaken to catalogue the vast numbers of different images, from tribes far and wide, which had by now come into Murgatreud's possession.

He was exercised at the moment with the fascinating matter of classification. Any group of objects (or facts or people) can be subdivided in an infinite variety of ways.

Good ways will bring together in each sub-group objects which have a genuine affinity, and will leave no objects with nowhere to go. Bad ways lead to strange bedfellows and a refugee problem.

Manning was acutely aware that he had here a chance to make a lasting mark in the academic world. By a lucky accident he was the man on the spot. Like one of the writers who happened to accompany Pizarro into the land of the Incas, like a traveller who might have noted down in his diary a visit to the Globe Theatre, his words, from the actual scene of the event, would have an authority which no one else, however booklined his Oxford study, could quite hope to match. His classification, if it was even half way competent, would remain *the* classification of the pygmy images.

Lost in his thoughts, he had allowed the temperature to rise slightly too high for comfort (97·5°, said the thermometer, still erect in his navel), but when he transferred his toes from the hot to the cold tap only a dribble of brown water came out.

'J.K.,' he called, 'more water in the cold tank.'

'Water along cold tank,' yelled J.K. 'No water along hot tank till sahib along out.'

Almost immediately Manning heard buckets of water going into one of the two cisterns (the whole arrangement was a more streamlined version of Murgatreud's original flush toilet, with a baked-earth stove under the hot tank), and soon the cold tap spluttered and coughed and the mercury sank again to 95·5°.

Manning had first tried classification of the images by geographical territories, but had long ago rejected this. To define the boundary of a territory he had had to fix upon some type of stylistic distinction between it and its neighbour, and any such distinction immediately fragmented the neat geographical shapes he had in mind. Classification according to materials (gold, wood, feathers) had led to no very recognizable groupings, nor had an attempt to attach European labels to the differing images, dubbing them variously Mannerist, Abstract, Baroque or Brutalist.

It was in his bath two nights ago, at about 94·9°, that the moment of breakthrough had occurred: in a primarily phallic art form, the classifying feature must clearly be the phallus. This simple illustration had led to startling results. The groupings which emerged did not conform to any solid territorial blocks, as in his original conception, but they did make shapes with long arms reaching out from a centre, like extremely fey pieces of jigsaw. This pattern of cultural development Manning had already decided to define, in his first article on the subject, as 'contiguous but non-continuous'. Now, as he gently arched and then lowered his spine to send water sucking and gurgling between his arms and ribs, he was pondering the delightful matter of naming these very satisfactory new classifications. He had last night decided to borrow a leaf from the ethnologists, who class all humanity as either brachycephalic (having short broad heads) or dolichocephalic (long narrow heads). Every pygmy image, according to the comparative length and breadth of the erect penis, was to be either brachyphallic or dolichophallic. The next stage was to label the various subdivisions of these two major categories. Swilling pleasantly around Manning's steam-filled mind were such possibilities as Biscuit Tin Culture and Door Knob Culture (brachyphallic) and Wand Culture, Thistle Culture and Barley Sugar Culture (dolichophallic, which in the circumstances was far the larger group).

Manning rose at last from the hot bath, savoured the brief moment of near black-out which proved that the arteries were not yet irretrievably hardened, and dried himself with some irritation on one of the new towels which had not yet been washed and appeared to be positively water-resistant. After dressing in comfortable slacks, and sprinkling on his hair a few drops of Mr Trumper's special mixture (a favourite luxury which he had once mentioned to Murgatreud, with now predictable results), he gathered up J.K. and headed into the treasury to continue the good work.

The treasury was a tower in the smithy compound. It was open to the sky, but a sloping roof round the inside, a little above head height, protected the curving shelves on which the images were stacked. Manning undid the padlock on the door (with the only duplicate key which Murgatreud would entrust to other hands), and settled himself at his desk, opening the large leather ledger which was to be the basis of his great catalogue. Ruler, callipers, set square and three sharp pencils were arranged in a neat row. J.K. stood beside him and held out for his inspection, much as a waiter does a bottle of wine, a lovely golden image about fifteen inches high. The sun slanted in through the open roof and reached just low enough to catch a few objects near the edge of a shelf and set them aglow. Specks of dust drifted lazily through it, motes in the yellow beam. It could have been an early Flemish painting of a merchant and his man.

Manning entered in the ledger a general description of the object, with details of the materials used, while J.K. took its height, breadth and depth in centimetres, followed by the corresponding measurements of the phallus and its angle of incidence, or Jut Factor. From these figures would come the object's final classification.

'Particularly beautiful one, that,' said Manning.

'Rather better than old Epstein, I imagine,' said J.K., with an odd hint of arrogance in his voice. Manning had always encouraged the boy's pride in his own race, but in due proportion.

'Granted,' he said, 'but even so, I'd trade you fifty of these for one Praxiteles.'

'I was thinking more of the old country.'

'Oh well, there's always . . .'

'Such as who?'

Manning was irritated at not being able to think of a single British sculptor whom he could admire, and this irritation led to his producing an argument of Murgatreud's. He pointed to the only incongruous objects in this golden treasure-house, the three machine-guns which stood clipped by their necks to the edge of a shelf with their ammunition coiled in metal boxes at their feet.

'There are parts of those things,' he said, 'as beautifully made as anything here. I'll show you.'

Having mastered under Murgatreud's tuition the first stage of dismantling, Manning was able to extract with three deft movements the bolt of the gun, the small gleaming shuttle which ran back and forth in its groove, collecting and discharging each successive round. It was indeed a beautiful object. The lines and hollows looked so perfectly precise in every detail. Its gleaming flank seemed slippery as much with its own immaculate smoothness as with the thin layer of oil which coated it. Manning handed the bolt to J.K.

'Feel that.'

'Very nice. But is it really as good as these images? I mean I'm asking, that's all.'

Manning smiled. This was still his pupil, the standards were still his. 'Well, since you're asking. I would say no, it's not. Come on, let's put it back.'

This proved easier said than done. Amazingly, the last stage of assembly appeared not to be the same as the first stage of dismantling in reverse. There was a knob at one end. With the knob inclined to the right, the bolt fitted in easily but fell out again as soon as the gun was lifted vertical. With the knob inclined to the left, no amount of shoving and grunting would persuade the vile little object back into its nice smooth channel. Manning's response to the crisis was unimaginative. When both systems had failed, his solution was to try one of them again, and then to try the other. Again and again the bolt fell out. Again and again it refused to go back in.

After about five minutes Murgatreud was heard outside in the smithy, discussing with Dong and Ding the latest requirements in the arms race. Manning by now showed signs of panic, and J.K. took over the struggle. He was bolder in his approach and made a series of adjustments in the breech of the gun before trying to fit the bolt back into it. Soon he found the right combination and the bolt slid casually home, so free and easy now that the solution seemed to have been obvious all along.

By the time Murgatreud did finally amble in, with a genial 'So howsda professorey?', Manning and J.K. were safely on their knees bedding the most recently classified images deep in cotton wool in reinforced crates, in which they were soon to be helicopted out to the art markets of the West. But Manning's heart was pounding as if he were the schoolboy.

XXV

A magnificent phallus rose from the head of Chief Alalo, as proud and poignant as the horn on a rhinoceros.

Alalo's tribe had by now acquired a very special status. What with providing blacksmiths, medical orderlies, itinerant friars, instructors in pidgin English, nurses, the Tiny Sisters of Mercy and the large labour force required for all the works of construction, they had no one left with any time to practise warfare. Soon, for such unrewarding tasks as felling and carting bamboo, they began to employ unskilled labour from other villages. At the craftsman level, among an emerging middle class, their tribe was growing rapidly by marriage. Talented young men from outside – people who had already distinguished themselves, perhaps, in single combat or by their understanding of scripture – were now eager to marry among them. To do so was like entering a secure and noncelibate priesthood, or going into the civil service. By the mere presence of Murgatreud and the stream of visitors who came to do business with him, Alalo's village had become the capital of the territory. And prosperous in proportion.

But if there was no longer a need for the tribe to do any fighting, this is not to say they required no new armour. There was still a considerable supply of golden images in

Alalo's secret store-house, and a capital city requires a certain amount of ceremony. As Murgatreud pointed out to old Alalo, the honour of providing ceremonial troops must surely fall to him.

Ceremonial troops need ceremonial armour, and ceremonial armour is, unfortunately, expensive. It always has been. There was a section of the subject in *Der Waffenschmied*, showing magnificent painted helmets surmounted by proud three-dimensional crests, dolphins' heads in crowns, unicorns rampant or pelicans pecking blood from their own breasts. For the ceremonial armour of Alalo and his men there was one obviously appropriate crest, in spite of spirited opposition from Father O'Halloran.

In return for many more golden images, Murgatreud adapted the tribe's own phallic extravaganzas to the requirements of a helmet. With such extra details as crimson paint, or with cassowary feathers taking their natural place both as a puff of joy and an ordinary old plume, he had soon forged phalli of sufficiently varied shape, size, colour and texture to fill a medium-sized Freudian notebook. And, very properly, the largest and strongest and brightest and fluffiest was the one that rose confidently from the brow of Chief Alalo.

XXVI

The Sundowner Bar is just one of many on the waterfront in Port Moresby, but has raised itself a cut above the rest by installing a carpet, Muzak and a special soft form of P.V.C. upholstery which, in the dim light, passes easily for leather. Ted Colloni, when he got back early from a job, liked to meet his friends here of an evening. As they worked mostly in offices, whereas he flew a contract helicopter (a service much in demand in New Guinea's rugged and undeveloped countryside), his stories tended to be better than most, and tonight was no exception.

'I tell you,' he said, 'I could hardly believe me eyes. I saw their smoke signal far away, so I come in low over the trees to a clearing by a river. Then I look down, and what do I see? Three whiteys looking up at me, well that's a common enough view of humanity for a chopper pilot' ('Get away' said one of his friends, without disturbing the rhythm), 'and then a whole bunch of niggers staring up too, and a long row of bright tin cans. So I think to myself, they've tried to give me some kind of landing aid, something I never do need, so down I come. And I get the shock of me life. I tell you, those weren't tin cans. Those were bleeding little pygmies, smallest little blokes you ever did see. And they were wearing bleeding armour. Yes they were. Like the shining white knight on the box. And you know another thing, you know what those little blokes had on their heads? They had bleeding great erections on their heads. Yes, erections, Charlie. That is not an ill-chosen word in the circumstances, Charlie. I chose it, Charlie. They had erections. Out of the top of their heads. Bleeding great erections,' and he gestured to underline his meaning.

A bar is the natural home and proper resting-place for tall stories. Here even the Anthropophagi, who carry their heads under their arms, would be soberly received. Charlie bought him another drink.

'I almost hopped back in and away. Then this bloke, fattest fellow you ever did see – all right, Charlie, one of the fattest – in white shorts he was, you know, pith helmet, and he had two others with him, and they took me into a sort of fort, little bleeding wooden fort, and they gave me, you'd never guess, no, you won't, don't try, glass of coconut milk. Would you believe it?'

('We shall give him a glass of brandy, I suppose?' Manning

had asked, in advance. 'Nottonya nellie,' was Murgatreud's reply, 'schmuck flies wid my stuff, milk.')

'So these little black newts loaded the crates into the bleeding chopper, and off I went, sooner the better, gave me the creeps.'

'What was in them?'

'Bleeding little doll things. Looked like gold.'

'Gold?'

There was renewed interest in the bar.

'Fat bloke had gone down to see the things put in the chopper, and I was up there with a big lanky fellow, taller than Charlie, so I raised me glass of milk' (and here he raised his glass; 'Someone fill the poor bastard up at least,' said Charlie), 'and I said to him, what's in those bleeding, pardon the expression, crates, and he came back, real pommy talk, faint buzzing somewhere up here' (he pinched the top of his nose and made a rough shot at Manning's outdated vowels), ' "Well, as a matter of fact, they're some rather interesting local artefacts," artefacts, Charlie, and he went into a hut and brought out this bleeding little yellow doll, looked like gold to me, but what was funny, I said to the fat bloke just as I was clambering back in, I said what is this place, bleeding valley of the dolls? He didn't twig. So I said, in the crates, little golden dolls. And he looked surprised. He said no. Botanical specimens, he said.'

'Well, where are the crates? See for ourselves.'

'Can't.'

'Why not?'

'Sealed.'

'Easy. Where are they?'

'At the airport. Flying out tonight.' The pilot looked shakily at his watch in the dark bar. 'Probably gone.'

'Anyway, there's no bleeding gold in New Guinea.'

'Sure there is,' said Charlie.

'Gold in New Guinea?'

'Plenty. But only dust. And you'd never gather enough to stuff a whore, let alone a bleeding crate.'

And on this nostalgic note they had another round.

XXVII

The visit of the helicopter was the strongest proof yet, from the pygmies' point of view, of the real powers of Christianity. Yet it coincided almost exactly with what looked to the white men like the beginning of the end.

The pygmies were at last running out of golden images, and they had no reserves of dust to fashion more. Even worse, tribes were now being reached on the periphery of the territory who seemed never to have made a golden image. They were fiercer and better fighters than their neighbours nearer the centre, but now that those neighbours were armed they found themselves suffering unprecedented defeats. They came, like everyone else to Murgatreud, but they came without images. There was nothing he could do for them.

Clearly the area where gold was easily available in the rivers was a limited one, and only within it had the art of the pygmies flourished. Murgatreud's operation seemed almost over. It had reached its natural boundaries.

Manning provided the solution. 'We should,' he said, 'take a leaf out of the notebooks of the Italian city states.'

'Ja so,' said Murgatreud.

'As you will no doubt remember,' continued Manning, and Murgatreud was already nodding, 'by about the fourteenth century the city states of Italy had become so rich, so luxurious, that the young men were no longer prepared to submit themselves to the rigours of life on campaign. They were unwilling to fight the wars necessary to defend their cities. So they employed armies of mercenaries, the famous *condottieri*, to fight their battles for them, while they relaxed in a life of culture and ease, literature and art, poetry and courtly love.'

'History is wunderbar,' volunteered Murgatreud gloomily.

'You haven't understood. The tribes with the skill to make these images are our city states. Let them employ as mercenaries the tribes whose only skill is fighting. They will then be free to concentrate on making more images, to buy more armour, to equip more mercenaries. *Et cetera. Ad infinitum.*'

'Itsy-bitsy problem, amigo,' explained Murgatreud with weary patience, 'gold dust finito.'

'Fly some in.'

'Fly gold?'

'Why not? It's more valuable in the form of images than as plain ingots. Bring your raw materials to the manufacturing skill, and take the finished product to the best market. That's business.'

The doctor was learning fast, and by now he had interested his tutor.

'Hey, professorey,' said Murgatreud slowly, pressing the end of his pudgy nose with a fat, squashy finger, 'professorey, ya gotta point. Hot ferdomma, amigo, spot on.'

Two weeks later, the first gold bars were dropped in, together with a few sets of modern jeweller's tools to speed up the pygmy output.

A certain amount of persuasion was required. The pygmies loved fighting, especially in armour, and they had little interest in paying someone else to do it for them. The problem was solved by withholding the new supplies of gold from any tribe which insisted on buying armour for itself instead of for mercenaries. Thus only a tribe willing to employ mercenaries was able to buy the very latest in armour and weapons, and any tribe of craftsmen still attempting to do their own fighting soon found themselves at a serious disadvantage.

The savage tribes from the periphery fell in readily with Murgatreud's plans. It was their first and only chance to enter the system, already so profitable to all concerned. Like medieval freelances attending a military market, distant chieftains would arrive with a score of tiny black followers to report to Murgatreud in the fort, where they would be equipped with armour and weapons and then led off to their new masters. The mercenaries were paid by the tribe employing them. Only the money for the armour came to Murgatreud. And by this prudent outlay of funds, the craft tribes bought for themselves a period of peace and safety during which they could make, undisturbed, the artefacts which would provide for their peace and safety in the future.

'Anywhere else it would be known as a protection racket,' observed Manning.

'So everyone's happy,' said Murgatreud.

The new arrangements brought into clearer perspective the present nature of the pygmy economy. There were now two types of currency in use. There were the golden images, which had direct value only in transactions with the Europeans. And there were the cowrie shells, which always had been, and still were, the normal currency between the pygmies themselves. To add to the general impression of spiralling wealth and prosperity, Murgatreud imported five hundredweight of cowrie shells from a deserted beach in Australia. These were passed gradually into circulation by being paid to Chief Alalo and his men for their official services.

XXVIII

Wellington Drive crossed Eisenhower Avenue at something approaching a right angle, and Queen Elizabeth II Boulevard intersected both during its long winding course from the fort at one end to the similar but smaller palace occupied by Alalo on the other side of the town.

'So wassa matta if it don't go straight?' Murgatreud had

commented on the vagaries of the Boulevard. 'So wassa matta wid Broadway, huh?'

Unlike Broadway, neither the Drive nor the Avenue nor the Boulevard was more than five feet wide, but they were the principal thoroughfares of the chaotic township which had sprung up around Chief Alalo's village. It had grown in a manner as apparently haphazard as the movement of amoebas. Huts and shacks seemed to couple in the night, to merge and produce offspring, while others as inexplicably withered and vanished. People extended their rooms today into space that had yesterday been a public thoroughfare, and tomorrow a tumbledown dwelling on the other side of the road would be removed instead by the passing traffic. Even Queen Elizabeth II Boulevard altered course day by day as casually as a delta stream. The only rule was that nothing could be built within fifty yards of the fort. So the turmoil of native huts came to a neat and precise edge in an arc which ran exactly parallel to Murgatreud's outer wall with its three forbidding bastions.

In the majority of squalid dwellings lived the many artisans who had been brought in from other tribes to meet the needs of this hub of empire, while in a few considerably more lavish bamboo mansions, visible here and there in the sprawling township, dwelt the diplomats. Every tribe now found it politic to keep a representative close to the centre, and in direct touch with Murgatreud. Only thus could they hope to hear of the latest breakthroughs in the field of armaments. Only thus might they put in a bid before their rivals. Only thus could they get advance warning of the unprincipled skulduggeries contemplated by hostile factions.

From time to time Murgatreud would bring these representatives together in what he liked to call his parliament. They would assemble on the bare green knoll behind the fort, between church and hospital. Murgatreud presided in a purely advisory capacity, leaving the immediate control of the meeting to Alalo, who was led to a kind of woolsack by J.K. as Black Rod. Here, with the full paraphernalia of civilized debate, matters of non-partisan interest were discussed, matters which might bring benefit to the whole

III

territory. The language of the assembly was pidgin English – long established now as the only convenient means of communication among so many pygmy dialects. Motions were moved and seconded (the formula was a little unwieldy – 'Motion move along move one', 'Motion move along move two', 'Motion move along'), divisions took place, resolutions were passed. Everyone enjoyed it all immensely. And, as Manning and Murgatreud pointed out to each other, it was teaching the little blighters the basic principles of parliamentary democracy and a decent way of carrying on.

XXIX

It was at the head of one of the mercenary bands that the giant arrived. It was an ominous moment, dark with portent, striking primitive terror into the heart of every bystander, when he strolled into the fort as casually as if he were any other man and the day but a day of the week.

'God have mercy upon us,' said O'Halloran, and he had furtively crossed himself before he could suppress the instinctive reaction.

Murgatreud turned and let fall a breastplate that he was fitting to a mercenary. Gravity seized his jaw. Like a stranded fish, mouth open and eye glazed, he stared at the newcomer.

'I say, that's an awfully big chap,' said Manning.

Size, to adapt slightly the old essay subject, lieth in the eye of the beholder. An onion the size of a cabbage is enough to give a strong sense of hallucination. A flea as large as a ladybird would be a terrifying monster, a phenomenon, a scandal, whereas nothing is more charming and petite than a ladybird. Expectation is all. The giant was about five feet three inches high, it was later discovered, which made him admittedly nine inches taller than the average male pygmy, but still three inches less than the diminutive, tousle-headed O'Halloran. And between the giant erect and Manning stooping, the normal posture of each, there was almost a foot of distinction. Even so, everyone shuddered as he strolled casually into the compound. And rightly.

A few days later Goliath was fitted out with the biggest suit of armour that had ever been made, and was sent with his men into the service of a tribe which was a particular favourite of Murgatreud's. The simple design of their unusually large golden images was ideal for a quick and handsome profit on the ingots now being provided. They could afford a friend like Goliath.

XXX

There was hammering in every valley.

'Iron along red along colour man tongue punch along rivet hole, iron along black punch along rivet,' was the slogan which Dong and Ding taught when spreading the techniques of the forge through the pygmy tribes. Every village now had large piles of outdated armour, useless at the more recent levels of military sophistication, and Murgatreud encouraged the skills which would turn all this scrap-iron into pots and pans and ploughshares. This development marked the beginning of a native industry, and Murgatreud subcontracted to these new village smiths some of the simpler parts of his own manufacturing processes, so as to ease the pressure on Alalo's ever-growing capital city.

It was, Manning and Murgatreud would remark complacently to each other, the first real step towards independence. O'Halloran could occasionally be heard muttering about dark Satanic mills, but the others paid little attention. The priest had been moody of late. His permanently full cathedral, even the steady foundation of churches in other villages, no longer seemed to satisfy him.

The real dynamic of the enterprise now depended on Manning and Murgatreud alone.

XXXI

The trend in pygmy diplomacy was towards ever greater alliances, until eventually all the craft tribes had formed themselves into two massive confederations, each employing roughly half the available *condottieri*. And among the *condottieri*, corresponding to this need, two obvious leaders had emerged.

One was Goliath. His skill with every type of weapon was already legendary, and his strength was prodigious. He had driven the point of a lance through one of the pepper-pot eye-holes of a rival, enlarging the hole with the force of his thrust from the size of a grain of corn to that of a cherry. He had swung the barbed ball of a Holy Water Sprinkler with such gusto into an enemy's breastplate that the points snarled themselves in the metal and the victim swung back on the chain, as if stuck to a mighty burr. It had on occasions brought tears to the normally dry eyes of Murgatreud to see his weapons used with such prowess, tears which by surface tension had formed into one great bubble of water in the narrowing gap between each eyebrow and puffy cheek, and which had totally blurred his vision of the amazing Goliath until a handkerchief could be dragged out to devour the moisture.

The rival leader, at the head of the other confederation's forces, would be no match for Goliath in single combat. Yet he had a ferocity which might prove decisive in extremities. He was a genuine leader of men, whereas Goliath required no more than his great size to make soldiers follow him. He was also a considerably more subtle tactician. Naturally, he became known as David.

In a large pitched battle it was hard to tell which of the talents, Goliath's or David's, would prove more useful, and a pitched battle was the trial of strength towards which the two great alliances of tribes found themselves inexorably heading. Ever greater secrecy surrounded the sale of weapons. Both sides negotiated in the fort with Murgatreud, but there was strict security to ensure that neither knew what weapons had been offered to the other, or in what quantity, or at what price. And the weapons themselves were transported to the camps of the rival armies in sealed crates. Rumours, of course, flew in all directions. But how reliable were they? Who really had what? Only the event would tell.

XXXII

The battle was to take place about three miles from the fort in a natural clearing by the river, the only open space large enough for the purpose. The surrounding hills were crowned with the usual dense jungle, but the sides which sloped down to the flat area near the river were covered only in a short mossy grass clinging to the hard rock a mere inch below the surface. On a small promontory near the top of one of these slopes Murgatreud, Manning and O'Halloran had installed themselves to watch the proceedings. Far below them, on the other side of the tumbling river, groups of heavily armed mercenaries could be seen slowly arranging themselves in rectangular formations in the hot morning sun. Behind the battle-field rose another hill, balancing on that side of the river the one occupied on this by Murgatreud, with an open swathe sloping down between two wings of jungle, like a glacier which over the ages had formed the plain beneath.

The present position of the three Europeans in the landscape, raised high in the foreground with the dispositions of battle clearly visible beyond and below them, was precisely that of the general and his A.D.C.s in eighteenth-century paintings of great campaigns. But instead of being on horseback, telescope in hand and the map resting lightly on the animal's mane, Murgatreud and his two friends were sitting at their ease in folding chairs under a bright Indian canopy, supported at each corner by a bamboo pole and held with guy-ropes. They had moved out here soon after dawn, with the help of some twenty bearers. Behind them, a long collapsible aluminium table was spread with a white damask cloth, hanging near enough to the ground to hide the ungainly metal legs. And on the table were various snacks. There was a tin of *foie gras*. There were olives and artichoke hearts. There was an entire salami from Bologna, still wrapped in its silver paper. What looked like a chunk of Cheddar was in fact something rather more special, *oude kaas* or 'old cheese' from Amsterdam, a pungent product kept for years, increasing in value at compound interest, to which Murgatreud had always been partial. There was a pile of jumbo-sized *matzos*. As a special treat for Manning there was some Patum Peperium, or Gentleman's Relish, a shallow scoop of dark paste in a ponderous white pot with archaic lettering. And, of course, there was Napoleon brandy and *marrons glacés*.

Murgatreud was in an expansive mood. News had come that the first sale of images at Sotheby's and Parke Bernet had exceeded all expectation. Prices had been high and there was already a strong international demand for more. It was clear that the costs of the whole undertaking, enormous though they had been, could be recovered in the not-too-distant future. Then money would begin to flow again into that numbered bank account in Geneva.

'Must be a tidy sum in that account already,' commented Manning in a genuinely neutral voice.

Murgatreud looked pleased but secretive. 'Mebbe so. Mebbe no. But mebbe so.'

'What are you going to do with it all,' asked O'Halloran, 'so much money as that?'

Murgatreud flicked open his right hand and held up his palm towards the priest (a gesture of slightly pained dissent which he had picked up in India). Then he placed the hand reverently on his heart. He was refuting any implication, however unspoken, that he might possibly, a man such as he, be remotely interested in storing up money for himself.

'Gimme da simple life. Travel, work, sleep, work, travel. So wenta spend? Bitta food mebbe, ristorante simpatico, sippa cognac, marron glacé. Bas. Basta. Gimme da simple life.'

There was a pause. Manning and O'Halloran nodded sympathetically. Murgatreud looked humble and contented.

'So what are you going to do with it all,' repeated O'Halloran, 'so much money as that?'

Murgatreud replaced his hand on his heart and began to appear positively maudlin.

'Ya wanna know?'

'Yes,' said O'Halloran.

'Wouldn't wish to intrude, of course,' put in Manning.

'Nana. Ya wanna know?'

'Yes,' said O'Halloran.

Murgatreud closed his eyes, covering them with a barely

perceptible movement of the encroaching flesh. After a pause they peeped out again.

'Da liddel childern,' he said, and let his head flop to one side. He spoke slowly. 'Liddel chiidern no chowda, liddel childern big pot, liddel childern no mama, liddel childern no legs, no arms, no apartment, like mebbe boils, like worms. Big eyes, liddel schmucks. Love 'em all. Liddel childern all kindsa problems.'

There was a silence.

'And ... and ... you mean you're going to use all that money in Geneva to help the little children?' said O'Halloran.

Murgatreud gave a lugubrious nod.

'But that's beautiful.'

The philanthropist looked moist and moody, and once again replaced the hand which had strayed from his heart. 'Big heart. No friends. Work, work, work, no time fa friends. No friends, no mama, no hausfrau, no bambini, no ciao, no arrivederci. So. Da liddel childern.'

This confession somewhat embarrassed the other two. They hastened to contradict his assessment.

'Oh, surely, come, come,' said Manning, 'you must have friends, a man like you.'

'Na.'

'One or two, here or there.'

'Na.'

'Someone in New York, maybe?' suggested O'Halloran.

'Na.'

'Paris? Johannesburg? The Côte d'Azur?'

'Na.'

'What about the Contact?'

'Never met da guy.'

'Oh.'

O'Halloran suddenly had a brainwave. 'Well, you have two friends at least.'

'So who?'

'Us.'

'Grazie, grazie,' said Murgatreud, and he pressed each of them by the hand, adding, as if to clinch the deal, 'amigos.'

'And the little children shall gain by your loss, I see the hand of God in that.'

'Oh, certainly,' said Manning, 'look at it that way.'

So Murgatreud went on to explain how one day soon, when he was passing through Geneva, he would choose some suitable organization, some charitable trust which could see that the money got to the little children, and he would confide to that organization the valuable secret, the number for withdrawing money from his numbered bank account, so that if anything should ever happen to him . . .

'God forbid,' said O'Halloran.

And deep inside him Murgatreud felt sure that He would.

The mention of his own charitable intentions had plunged Murgatreud into a mood of sentimental gloom, but the start of the battle soon snapped him out of it. The two armies consisted of many smaller tribal groups, each under its own local chieftain but all accepting the ultimate authority of either David or Goliath. They had formed up in separate phalanxes all over the field and they now moved slowly into a series of prolonged clashes. From above, each encounter between a pair of metal-clad squads looked as though two blobs of mercury were being drawn slowly towards each other to merge, by some instant chemical reaction, into one seething mass. On the ground, such a confrontation immediately degenerated into dozens of single combats. Since two knights could easily get the better of one, the generals had to ensure that at no part of the field were their men likely to be outnumbered.

It was a hot day, and soon the three distinguished spectators felt in need of refreshment. The cognac was circulating, and the *foie gras* has just been broached, when Goliath scored the first advantage. One large group of brawling knights had drifted by some inner momentum close to the jungle at the edge of the field of battle, when suddenly there emerged from the trees a posse of nimble men wearing no armour at all. Instead they carried long metal flails, whose heavy ends, swinging viciously from the joint, could outreach the sword of an armoured knight. A blow from these could knock a man sideways, and if aimed at the back of the knees would invariably bring him down. Relying on speed alone, the skirmishers dashed round the outside of the mass of struggling humanity, directing well-aimed blows at any of the enemy who were projecting from the scrimmage.

But the *foie gras* was scarcely half finished before David turned the tables. A group of equally unarmed men appeared on his behalf wielding long whips, splayed for the last two feet of the lash into five separate thongs, each of which ended in a metal tip. These could far outreach the flails and they bit with devastating effect into the unarmed flesh of the flailers. In that part of the field, Goliath's chances suddenly looked slim.

Murgatreud was very eager that Manning and O'Halloran should sample the *oude kaas*, and he was delighted when they pronounced it excellent. He was also most gratified when they noticed and were impressed by the wide range of new weapons appearing on the field as the battle progressed. It was amazing, they all readily agreed, what incredible progress had been made in the comparatively short time (a little under three years) since Alalo had first demanded the suit of armour made for Dong.

All day the tide of battle ebbed and flowed. When O'Halloran discovered an unsuspected passion for black olives, Goliath's star was once again in the ascendant. He himself had been visible, achieving wonders with his own version of the Holy Water Sprinkler, developed for him personally by Murgatreud. It had a heavier head and a longer chain than anyone else's, but the points were blunted so as to dent but not penetrate a rival's breastplate. Swinging the great ball on the end of its chain, Goliath could at times be seen to knock down, on a ninepins principle, four or five closely bunched enemies with a single blow.

But then again, by the time Manning was finally persuaded to break the seal on the Patum Peperium, a delicacy which always reminded him of tea beside a blazing fire after the wall game on November afternoons at Eton, David had recovered much of his lost advantage by a classic flanking manoeuvre worthy of a Marlborough or a Wellington. From above, when compared to the dashing wheel of a squadron of cavalry David's slow deployment round the field of a company of heavily armoured foot-soldiers had an agonizingly ponderous quality. It seemed inconceivable that such a lengthy move should pass unnoticed. But Goliath was too busy laying about him to suspect anything so intellectual, and at last David's men had established a clear superiority of nearly three to one in a distant corner of the field and were inflicting some very heavy damage. The little Red Cross orderlies from Alalo's tribe could be seen dashing in and out of the trees with their stretchers, but they could hardly keep pace with requirements.

By mid-afternoon, when the damask table-cloth was stripped almost bare, Goliath's men were behaving in a very strange fashion. They seemed no longer to try to win the fight, but merely to confine it to a central area of the field. By means of each group steadily retreating before its rivals – from above it looked as though they were towing them about – they gradually contrived things so that David's men were clustered in the middle of the field, at the foot of the steep hill, in an apparently solid and victorious phalanx.

Only Murgatreud knew what this tactic was leading to. The tribes backing Goliath had outbidden their rivals in the negotiations leading up to the battle, and it was to them that Murgatreud had sold his most spectacular weapon, a device of which he was justifiably proud. Throughout the entire arms race up to this point he had been handicapped by one inescapable fact: the bulk of medieval European armour was designed for horsemen, and there were no horses in New Guinea. The essential striking power of a medieval knight – the thrust of a lance with the full momentum of a horse behind it – was barred to the pygmy warriors. They had been limited, until this battle, to the repertoire of the foot-soldier, who has played in the annals of armoured men a very second-ary role. Murgatreud's solution, his break-through, had been to substitute for the muscle of a horse the power of gravity.

He knew full well why Goliath was gathering his enemies at the bottom of the hill, and soon the six secret machines appeared from among the trees at the top. Each was a cross between a bicycle and a small steamroller. On each, astride the bar between the broad metal wheels, sat a pygmy knight puffed up in armour, like a carnival king of excess, with a heavy lance tucked under his arm. The gradient was sufficient for these contraptions to accelerate at a most alarming speed. One hit a bump, and the knight went over the handlebars, landing with a metallic clang slightly to one side and continuing his progress down the hill roughly parallel to his machine. Another seemed to have a locked wheel, and traced an acute but even curve before plunging back into the jungle with a muffled splintering of wood. But the remaining four came on apace towards the terrified horde of David's men, huddled directly in their path at the bottom of the hill. In so far as they were able to run, they ran. Several were mowed down. Others leapt in their full armour into the river, where at least one of the contraptions followed them, totally out of control. But the psychological effect was even more important than the physical damage. The battle was clearly over. The day belonged to Goliath.

'A mystery weapon *par excellence*,' said Manning.

'Now, do you not think that's going a bit far?' fretted O'Halloran.

But Murgatreud brushed aside the hint of an objection, and urged them both to knock back the cognac as it was time to be off. He signalled the servants to dismantle the awning and pack up the picnic. It had been an extraordinarily pleasing demonstration. Now everyone would want a jousting bicycle.

XXXIII

That J.K. should have vanished for two days was bad enough. It was considerably worse when it was discovered where he had been.

He had been in the camp of the victorious Goliath, a champion who had lost much of his popularity in the fort by his behaviour in the few weeks since his great victory. He had mercilessly plundered many of the richest villages in the losing confederation, in spite of Murgatreud's express instructions that they should be allowed to pay their reparations in an orderly manner through his central agency. And he had turned a deaf ear to various summonses to present himself at the fort. Murgatreud bitterly regretted having given the jousting bicycle to such an unstable, indeed ungrateful, character.

And this was the unsavoury company which J.K., a man in an intimate position of trust at the very centre of affairs, had been keeping. Murgatreud was determined that he should be severely punished. He even talked of a public example. Faced with such extreme alternatives, Manning felt compelled to agree in principle that punishment was deserved; but this enabled him to insist that it should be, as it always had been, a private matter between J.K. and himself.

So for the last time a new bamboo cane was cut, and the Old Etonian and the well-spoken pygmy set out together into the jungle. Their traditional little clearing, reserved for this purpose, had been engulfed by the township. With some difficulty another was found – not quite as densely enclosed as might have been wished, not quite as secret and secure, but probably just safe enough for just long enough. And there, once again, after a gap of many years, J.K. received six.

But somehow they were no longer of the best. The savour had gone out of the ceremony. It was not only that the milieu was different, not only that Manning found it necessary to keep one eye over his shoulder in case of accidental intruders. It was that J.K. behaved now with a cheerful insolence, almost indeed a complete detachment, which was so very different from the mood of reverence and respect which he had once shown in similar circumstances.

When it was over, the Englishman tried to get back on a more familiar footing.

'Now come on, J.K.,' he said, 'come on now, we two understand each other, so tell me straight, why did you do it? Why on earth did you do it, J.K.?'

'Well, look at it my way, old chap,' came the reply – and that was already shock enough for a week – 'look at it my way. If you'd been a Philistine, and if Goliath, one of your own people after all, had said in a friendly way, why not pop round some time for a chat ... would you have said no?'

But the answer was a little too glib to be entirely satisfactory.

XXXIV

Three nights later, J.K. disarmed Murgatreud by a device which occupied a favourite little niche in Manning's gossipy view of English history.

In about 1670 (as Manning had often told J.K., each of them finding the story pleasantly saucy), Nell Gwynn's position as mistress and plaything to Charles II had been threatened by another Drury Lane actress, Moll Davis, whose charms had struck the monarch on several successive evenings as he sat in his box at the theatre, and whose coy and winsome trick of aiming any faintly ambiguous lines in the royal direction had seemed to Nell positively sick-making in its vulgarity, and her friends all agreed. But Moll made progress, and soon she was alternating with Nell in the royal bed. After a few weeks of this intolerable state of affairs, Nell found a solution – either from a dusty old manuscript, or from a lady of hideous mien, much like a witch and with warts on her chin, who kept a stall at the corner of the Lane (the records differ). Anyway, in accordance with the roughly scrawled prescription which Nell now carried in her bosom, she one evening concocted a jalap, or *purga de Jalapa*, for Moll. Moll was due to spend that night with the king, and the jalap was the most powerful purgative known to the seventeenth century. The potion was mixed backstage into the strong tot of rum with which Miss Davis liked to fortify herself between the fifth act of the comedy and the first of the romance. It had spectacular effects. The monarch soon grew impatient with a mistress who at every tenderest moment would leap suddenly from the bed, clasp her petticoats tight about her thighs, and hobble squawking down the passage to the privy. So good King Charles was faithful for ever after to pretty Nell, the darling of England, from a humble background, who founded the Royal Hospital at Chelsea.

The traditional magic of the pygmies was well able to provide J.K. with a suitable potion. The meal that evening was a prawn curry, merely the tin which Teresa happened to have opened. Murgatreud was now always waited on first, and before handing round the large plate J.K. mixed his brew into the area from which, as he knew by experience, Murgatreud would scoop a healthy portion. By an adroit turning of the dish. Manning and O'Halloran could be saved from too devastating an effect.

The reason for all this melodrama was that Murgatreud slept with two crucial items under his pillow – his revolver, loaded with its full complement of six bullets, and the chain of keys to different parts of the fort. These keys were in his pocket all day, with the chain anchored by a slit tongue of leather to one of the buttons of his shorts. The only time they were at all vulnerable was at night.

J.K. slept on the ground outside Manning's hut, and within half an hour he had the pleasure of hearing the first effects of his potion. With a muffled hot ferdomma, which itself seemed to burst through tightly pursed lips, Murgatreud shot from his hut and moved with unprecedented agility across the open space to the flush toilet. There followed the most gratifying explosions. J.K. smiled up at the stars, and waited. For his own security he wanted to analyse the pattern of the event. He discovered that absolute silences, some of them surprisingly long, separated the brief eruptions – whereas a period of heavy breathing led up to the moment when Murgatreud, exhausted and amazed, ambled back to the brief haven of his bed.

J.K.'s schedule for each subsequent visit was carefully planned. As soon as Murgatreud left his hut for the second time, J.K. nipped in behind him, quick as a shadow, and took the keys from under the pillow. In spite of the darkness, and a wide variety of possible choices for each padlock, he had opened the door into the smithy compound, and then the door to the treasury itself, and had returned the keys to their hiding-place before Murgatreud's spasm was over.

Murgatreud pulled the chain three times in rapid succession and was answered only by the hollow mocking sound of an empty cistern. Cursing in all the assembled tongues of Europe, he stumbled over to where J.K. lay and stubbed five soft toes purposefully into the pygmy's flank:

'Water, boy.'

J.K. experienced a fierce ironical delight in topping up the cistern, ready for the next bout, while his victim tried to get comfortable once more in bed. He even felt moved to place a couple of full buckets beside the pan, anticipating with some pleasure the later stretches of the night.

During Murgatreud's third spell, J.K. returned to the treasury and deftly removed the bolts of the three machine-guns (a thousand times in his mind, since that afternoon with Manning, he had repeated this routine). Then he gathered up the revolver from under the pillow and crossed to the gate in the outer wall of the fort. Slowly, to avoid a tell-tale squeak, he drew back the heavy bar. The great hinges of looped vine groaned slightly as he nudged open the door.

He sped through the unusually quiet township to the river. There he turned upstream, and slackened his pace. As he walked towards his meeting place with Goliath, he flung the three bolts, each one separately, far out into the rapids. The revolver he decided to keep, though he would tell Goliath that it too had gone into the river. It might come in handy later on as a symbol of authority.

XXXV

Arriving back in his bed for the third time within less than two hours, limp, exhausted, literally drained of strength, Murgatreud plunged his hand under the pillow for the reassuring feel of at least one unchanged part of his daytime self, a touch of solidity, of strength, of normality. His fingers closed on nothing. Groping to the right they found his keys. Jerking back from that position they lunged further up, hurried to the left, down, round the keys, back. Nothing. With what felt like a great electric charge somewhere just above his shattered bowels, Murgatreud's strength was back. He leapt out of bed, flicked off the pillow by one corner, groped again, reached at the same time with the other hand for his chunky explorer's torch, and jabbed the strong beam straight at the patch of crumpled sheet, behind the bed, beside the bed, under the bed, below the sheets. Nothing. He stormed out of the house to kick J.K. awake. Nothing.

He hurried on to where Teresa lay, outside O'Halloran's hut, and shining the beam in the girl's face he shook her by the shoulder, muttering all the time, 'Where J.K.? Where J.K.?' The girl slept with the heaviness of twenty-two years. He had shaken her again, even more roughly, before she rose suddenly on one elbow, with a look of terror, shielding her eyes from the beam.

'Where J.K.?'

'J.K.?'

'Where J.K.?' He shook her again.

'In bed, sahib.'

'Dumbkopf.'

'What the devil's going on?' Manning, in striped pyjamas identical to Murgatreud's except in girth, stepped unsteadily from his hut.

'Boy stole revolver. J.K. Scarpered, da schmuck.'

'Good God. How could he? I thought it was under your pillow.'

'Kinda rough night, ya mebbe heard, na?' said Murgatreud, with more than a trace of irritation.

'Yes, I had noticed. You sure you haven't mislaid it? Didn't leave it in the loo or something?'

But Murgatreud was adamant. 'Schmucklein stole,' he said, and he gave an admonitory kick at Teresa to emphasize his feelings.

'Steady on, old chap. Don't panic. If he did, he must be around somewhere. Gate's shut, isn't it?' And lifting his face a fraction towards the stars, Manning called out into the night. 'J.K. J.K. Where are you? Enough is enough, after all.'

O'Halloran had slipped on his cassock to confront the crisis. 'Mother of Mercy, what's the shamozzle about at this time of night?' he said, appearing in his doorway. 'Is the boy missing? Don't cry, child, don't cry, we'll find him easy,' and he was down on his knees to comfort Teresa.

A horrifying thought struck Murgatreud. 'Machine-guns,' he said, and dashed off towards the smithy compound.

'I'll check the gate,' volunteered Manning. He shuffled off rather more slowly in the direction of the main entrance, concentrating on keeping on his slippers, which had no backs.

'Open, Chrissake,' cried Murgatreud as he reached the door into the smithy compound, and he was half way towards the treasury when, with a sudden hot ferdomma, he abruptly changed course just in time to regain the privy.

'Gate's open, bird must have flown,' reported Manning. and then added, 'probably just a prank.'

'Prank baloney,' came from the privy, among other explosions. 'Check machine-guns.'

'Right-ho, but do keep calm,' said Manning, and he made his measured way through the smithy and into the treasury. 'No need to fret,' he called out, 'they're all here.'

'Treasury open?'

'Treasury open, yes. Funny, I admit, but maybe he took one or two of the new images. We've had some nice things in lately.'

As soon as he was free, Murgatreud joined Manning in the treasury. He shone his torch on the three guns. 'Eyes, dumbkopf, so wadya got eyes for, schmuck?' he yelled, and gave Manning a shove.

'Now look here, steady on, Murgatreud,' and this from Manning was a strong rebuke, 'I'm getting a bit sick of this, I can tell you. There they are. What's wrong?'

'Bolts? Ya see da bolts?' queried Murgatreud with mock patience. 'Huh? No bolts, no guns. Kaput.'

The discovery that the bolts were missing did, even Manning and O'Halloran were prepared to admit, put a more serious complexion on the matter.

'Schmuck forgot one liddel thing,' said Murgatreud with some satisfaction. 'Schmucklein forget emergency kit.'

He returned to his hut, chose a key from the ring which still lay exposed on the sheet and pulled out from under his bed the original emergency kit which had been salvaged from the wreck of his plane. Inside was the small black automatic, the coiled belt of bullets and the boxes of spare ammunition, numbering perhaps a hundred shots in all. Now that his anger could express itself in useful action again, Murgatreud became more calm. As he loaded the weapon he muttered to himself, almost with a fierce joy, 'Get da bum, get him one, two, three, four, five, six, ja.' The automatic was hardly an adequate replacement for the machine-guns. It was designed more for boudoir work than for withstanding a siege, but it could kill a man at the range of a few yards, and wing him at fifty. Knowing the terror the pygmies had always shown at the effect of a bullet, it might well be enough to restore discipline.

Armed with his powerful torch and the automatic, and delayed only by one more visit to the privy, Murgatreud finally stormed out of the fort and across to the first big hut on the edge of the township, fifty yards away. There, in the best tradition of Westerns, he leant back and kicked open the frail bamboo door. The hut was empty. So was the next. And the next. The entire seething township was deserted.

Murgatreud insisted that they should spend the rest of the night at action stations, even though Manning said that pygmies had never been known to attack in darkness. The bar was replaced on the outer gate, and the machine-guns were heaved up into the three bastions which faced the township – in the hope that the sight of their projecting muzzles would convince the pygmies that the loss of the bolts had not crippled them. Murgatreud sat in the central bastion, slumped against the parapet like a bereaved peasant, nursing his automatic in the crook of his elbow. Teresa, still biting back tears, made a continuous chain of cups of tea. Manning paced slowly round and round the wall of the smithy, whistling tuneless variations on a long-lost theme. O'Halloran spent much of his time on his knees, but he was praying for strength, not relief.

Relief was more in Murgatreud's department. From time to time he clambered down to his transmitter and croaked into the night, again and again, in long spells of precisely repeated distress, without pausing for reply, MAYDAY MAYDAY SURROUNDED HOSTILE PYGMIES 7.76 SOUTH 142.4 EAST MAYDAY MAYDAY. He preferred not to ask himself what anyone who received his message could possibly do with it. It was reassuring to be, even if not actually in contact, nevertheless within the possibility of contact with the outside world. Alas *the* Contact, the Contact himself, Murgatreud's own, would not be listening for the troubles of CATT for another sixteen hours or so, the other side of a long, alarming day.

XXXVI

Murgatreud's message was picked up by one group of people who were not at all far away, only about six miles, but vertically. The attention of the crew of a transcontinental jet was briefly and pleasantly diverted from the dull routines of the flight.

The radio operator looked surprised, tuned his wavelength more finely, waited, and then looked even more surprised.

'Hey,' he said, 'I'm getting a guy who says he's at 7.76 South, 142.4 East, wait for it . . . being attacked by pygmies.'

There were guffaws of laughter round the flight-deck.

'That's roughly below us,' said the navigator, 'but it's impenetrable jungle half way up into the ruddy mountains and he claims to be there with a transmitter.'

'Nut case,' said the captain, 'some radio ham in Port Moresby who can't sleep. Tell him we love him.'

The others agreed.

'Wish him the top of the morning.'

'Send me a pygmy sheila for Christmas.'

'He'll never receive me,' said the operator. 'He's still transmitting. Talking all the time. Same thing again and again.'

'Hell with him,' said the captain, 'put him in the log anyway. Makes a change.'

XXXVII

The sky had all along looked bright above the dark mass of jungle. With dawn, the most perceptible difference came in the area of the township itself. Below the line of the trees a faint grey glow began to appear; at first a mere softening of the blackness, then a hint of solid shapes, of roofs which happened to slope at a certain angle, or of walls set in relief by a darker alley beyond, but they were shapes which shivered and cracked as soon as Murgatreud forced his tired eyes to interpret them more closely. Manning thought the pygmies would return at dawn, so Murgatreud paid a last-minute visit to the privy and strained hard to avoid a crisis at a more crucial moment. He achieved nothing. In such circumstances the bowels will not be dictated to. By the time he was back at his post, the township was perfectly clear — a watercolour only, in the most muted range of greys, but clear in every detail.

No one felt like breakfast, and the dawn dragged on. In the township nothing moved. Even Murgatreud's stomach seemed to have finally settled down. Only the birds-of-paradise swooped, as always, to and fro from the trees of the jungle, flashing in the early sun their green throats and chestnut wings. Some even flew over the fort, in and out of this strongly barricaded area, with the ease of complete detachment, absolute neutrality. The stillness became uncanny — even, surprisingly, almost boring. It made it hard to believe, every minute by slow minute, in the full seriousness of the situation. It made it hard to believe, on occasion, and specially for Manning and O'Halloran, that their predicament had any reality at all.

The silence was broken about two hours after dawn by a shrill yodelling, which began somewhere in the middle of the township, was instantly echoed away in the jungle to the left, then just behind the church, in another part of the township, very close now, back in the jungle, and so on until the entire landscape seemed to be pulsating between low and high notes. It was a sound that Murgatreud had not heard, at close quarters, since his first unforgettable glimpse of pygmy savagery.

Still no one had been seen, until J.K. stepped from behind one of the nearest huts at the edge of the township.

'Why don't you open ...' he began to shout, and then Murgatreud fired. But he had done so too quickly, it was the wrong range for the weapon. J.K. stepped back into the dense township. All that the shot had killed, instantly, was the mad chorus of yodelling. Silence returned.

Murgatreud loaded another bullet, from the belt which barely reached round his waist, and poked his head over the top of the bastion.

'See little schmuck?' he yelled. 'Gotta gun. Forgotta gun. Come out. Hands up 'n out. Mebbe treat ya good, real good, sure.'

But there was no response. The silence continued for another fifteen minutes, perhaps twenty, punctuated only by occasional brief orations from the head and sometimes shoulders of Murgatreud above the wall.

Suddenly the yodelling started again, and a moment later a great volley of arrows rose from among the huts of the township. High in the air they arched, stayed poised for a moment and then changed direction to rain their murderous barbs down into the fort. The walls and bastions were designed for direct fire, such as a gun might produce. They were no defence against an attack from above.

'Shields, smithy,' yelled Murgatreud, huddling as close to the wall of the bastion as his great bulk would allow, and Manning, noticeably faster than usual, collected three outdated metal shields, obsolete now even in pygmy warfare, from a pile in the smithy compound. These he managed to distribute before the next volley. Teresa was ordered to stay under the bed in O'Halloran's hut.

The racket outside was now continuous, and pygmy bowmen, leaping with excitement, would dash out from the cover of huts or jungle towards the wall of the fort on whichever side Murgatreud was not peering out below his shield. With his circle of tin held on top of his head he scuttled ceaselessly round the walkway joining the bastions, turning and spinning like a fat demented terrapin. The pygmies were clearly enjoying the game, dashing foward as soon as he left one part of the wall and then nipping back into cover again, with laughter and exaggerated signs of terror, when he reappeared. It was an adult-sized version of I'm the King of the Castle, Get Down You Dirty Rascal. But there were too many dirty rascals.

Murgatreud, with some skill, waited until an incautious group was close to the wall and then, at a range of only a dozen yards, chose his man and fired. He killed him, and the intention was that the shock would bring the tribes to their senses. But it was too late for any such psychological subtlety. Each of Murgatreud's hundred bullets could have taken a life and still the pygmies, in their present excitement, would have come on. Already another bunch was up against the far wall with a ladder.

'Don't shoot. It's too late. There's no point,' yelled Manning, holding his shield above him like an umbrella in the middle of the compound. But Murgatreud reached the top of the ladder and fired down its slope, killing two, before he pushed it away. Another group was up on the wall on the opposite side, and now they swarmed in like ants. Murgatreud shot two more as the crowd headed for the gate and pulled back the heavy wooden bar. He had only one more bullet in his revolver, and no time to reload. He kept it for whoever should be standing on the other side of the gate.

As expected, it was J.K. and beside him Goliath, with an arrow already drawn in his bow. Murgatreud raised his arm to fire. Did he hesitate which to choose? Or was he too slow? Goliath's arrow struck him in the fleshy part of his left shoulder, just outside the socket of the arm, and it hung there, sagging slightly from the horizontal, with its barb firmly embedded. Murgatreud dropped his revolver as he grabbed with his right hand to prevent himself falling into the yard below.

O'Halloran held his crucifix out towards the open gate through which the pygmies now rushed, but it failed to stem the tide. 'Bless you, my children,' he announced as they grabbed him.

'Are you sure this is entirely wise?' queried Manning, as a party of pygmies, on instructions from J.K., lifted him off his feet and placed him face down on the ground.

Soon all three Europeans were lying trussed, their ankles tied together and their wrists securely bound behind their backs. Three chairs were brought and they were heaved up on to them, legs straight out in front, arms over the back of the chair, as formal and helpless as a row of customers in a barber's shop.

'First aid along arm along sahib,' said J.K., and an orderly hurried up to treat Murgatreud's wound. Manning noticed with an unexpected twinge of pleasure the care with which the operation was carried out. The barb was forced through Murgatreud's blubber until it pierced the skin on the other side. There it was cut off and the arrow was withdrawn. A thorough cleaning of the wound and a quick dressing completed a perfectly acceptable job. The pain that it involved prevented Murgatreud from making any active intervention while it was going on, but as soon as it was safely dressed he tried to attract J.K.'s attention.

'Hey, amigo, dooadeal, you 'n me, na?' he called, and if he had had a hand free he would have beckoned the pygmy aside for a private chat between men of the world, to the benefit of both parties. 'No kiddin, ya done good today, great operation. You 'n me partners, na, howbowdat? Jes great. Now on ya run da place, howbowdat? Call my Contact tonight. Wadya need? Guns? Gold? Cognac? Ya name it, we got it. Dooadeal, na? C'mon.'

But J.K. and Goliath were moving towards the gate, and most of the pygmies followed them out through it. A handful only were left to guard Teresa, who had already made valiant efforts to defend the three Europeans. She now broke free again from her guards, indignantly flinging their hands off her arm, and brought the captives a glass of brandy which she held to each pair of lips in turn.

'Bless you,' said O'Halloran, 'you are a lesson to us all.'

Murgatreud gulped his brandy, his and Napoleon's, and returned to his theme. Twisting his neck stiffly to look at his companions, he pleaded. 'Ya tell him, na? Dumbkopf, schmuck, dat J.K., dunno wass good for him. Ya tell him, tell him dooadeal. So he go places. Talented boy. Na?' There was no answer from his two friends. He continued in a less positive vein, his voice quieter and lower. 'So wadda they do to us, huh?'

'Never fear, my child,' said O'Halloran, 'you are in the hands of the Lord,' advice that Murgatreud took visibly ill.

'Interesting question, though,' said Manning, 'what they are going to do with us.'

It was answered soon enough, when the crowd of pygmies returned. Dong and Ding were at the head of them, directing half a dozen porters who carried a gigantic metal pot. It was a patchwork affair, made like an old peasant quilt from the available odds and ends. The shape of individual breastplates and shields, the odd greave to fill a gap, and even what seemed to be half a flattened helmet, could all be separately identified by their slightly differing colours and textures, neatly beaten into a continuous curve and riveted together.

A joyous light had come into O'Halloran's eye.

'So waddya need big pot for, hot ferdomma?' shouted Murgatreud.

It was a full-bellied pot, with a slightly outward-turning lip – the traditional design for the purpose. 'Amazing how these folk traditions spread, without any apparent contact,' said Manning, in a gallant but vain attempt to break the tension.

The pot was designed to fit exactly on top of the circular cement wall of the forge. The fire would blaze beneath it, self-contained, and it could be blown to an intense heat by the original rotating fan. The three trussed victims were manhandled across the thirty yards from where they sat, and then, after a brief pause, were heaved up and over the brim. The pygmies chose the lightest first.

'Forgive them, Lord, they know not what they do,'

murmured O'Halloran, on the verges of ecstasy as they dropped him into the pot, vast and empty. There were three rings on the inside, not far from the bottom. To one of these the vine around the priest's wrists was firmly attached.

'J.K., J.K.,' Manning called to his pupil, standing a few yards away, as the group of porters returned to carry him to the pot. 'J.K., I do suggest that a little more thought should be given to this before any irretrievable step is taken.'

There was no answer. Nobody seemed to be paying much attention to them as individuals.

Another thought struck Manning just as they were trying to bend his legs to get them into the pot. One obvious ally was conspicuously absent. 'J.K.,' he called out, 'where's Alalo?'

J.K. turned and drew the edge of his index finger across the front of his neck.

'You can't be serious.'

The elegant pygmy nodded.

'That can hardly have been necessary.'

'Cruel to be kind. He would have turned the whole tribe against us. Avoid infinitely more bloodshed this way. Like, perhaps, doing away with Alcibiades the night before he desecrated the Hermae. You of all people should appreciate that.'

Moving Murgatreud was quite a problem. It was solved by two stout bamboo poles, one under his knees, the other between his arms and his back. The length of the poles meant that a far greater number of pygmies could lend a hand than would have been able to get a grip on his person. So, like a trussed pig, bouncing up and down against the flexing of the poles, he was carried to the pot. 'Lemme go, schmucks,' he yelled, kicking and struggling like a fat boy about to be ducked, 'lemme go.' And as they laboured to heave him into the pot, he pleaded with J.K., 'Now c'mon, J.K., serious a moment, dooadeal. Dooadeal widya, J.K. C'mon, see sense, amigo, see sense, dooadeal, na?' But after a prolonged and undignified struggle he was finally squashed down into the pot. His wrists, like those of his two colleagues, were attached to one of the rings near the bottom. Anchored in this way, they could only just raise their heads high enough to peer out over the rim.

Women arrived with pitchers of water. They poured it into the centre of the pot, a succession of thin jets curving down between the three faces. It felt pleasantly cool. Finally the level was raised so near the top of the pot that the occupants were forced to kneel rather than sit on the bottom if their mouths were to remain above the surface.

'Dooadeal, c'mon, chrissake, dooadeal,' burbled Murgatreud, while the water lapped the folds of his chin.

Teresa had grabbed a sponge from O'Halloran's hut, and now she tried to force her way through the crowd of pygmies to the side of the pot. 'I only want to comfort the gentlemen,' she insisted, but she was pushed and pulled, mercilessly shoved from one group to another, amid shouts of laughter, as she tried to make her way forward. At one point she stumbled and fell, and two young men drew applause by jumping backwards and forwards over her body as she lay there.

'Stop along that,' said J.K. sharply. 'Let along alone.' So she came up to the pot and bathed the foreheads of the three men.

'Praise be to God,' said O'Halloran, 'my cup is full to overflowing.'

'Hardly the best chosen metaphor in the circumstances,' suggested Manning, but the priest was not to be deflected.

'My cup of joy is full to the brim,' he continued. 'In His infinite mercy God has granted me not only the joy of personal martyrdom, but the privilege and honour of helping another soul to the same heights. Bless you, my child, Teresa of the Little Way, for thou art a true and brave child of God.'

'Lemme out,' said Murgatreud, 'chrissake someone, dooadeal.'

XXXVIII

At this moment there appeared in the doorway of the compound a most improbable sight – a tall Australian with a sweat-streaked face, dishevelled khaki bush-shirt and shorts, and sandals on his bare feet. He looked exhausted. Long matted red hair hung down almost to his shoulders, and his bushy beard, of an even brighter hue, was tangled with burrs.

He supported himself with both hands against the doorposts as he took in the extraordinary sight which confronted him.

'Cheese and rice,' he muttered under his breath, like a man fingering a secret talisman in his pocket, and he tossed his head as if to shake the vision from his eyes.

'Cheese and rice,' he said again, with mounting urgency as he took in more of the scene.

Finally the full details of what he saw swept aside the coy rhyming circumlocution of his bourgeois Brisbane background, and he came out loud and clear with Australia's favourite phrase.

'Jesus Christ,' he said.

And the pygmies fell to their knees with one great murmur of assent: 'Alleluia.'

They bore him in triumph to a place of honour just opposite the other three white men, and they brought Murgatreud's great bamboo chair like a throne for him to sit on. Grabbing the sponge from Teresa, they dipped it in the water of the pot, which was already more than tepid, and gently bathed his tired face, his grimy hands torn by the jungle briars, even his hard and callused feet, which some of them attempted to dry with their bushy mops of hair, ill-designed for the purpose.

'Hey, fella. Gemme outa here, quick,' shouted Murgatreud, just keeping his face above the surface of the water.

'Do what I can, digger. Give me time. Looks as though these little fellows can turn nasty. Way I see it there's room in that pot for a fourth.'

'Frankly, from some points of view, time is what is rather limited,' suggested Manning.

'I know, I know, just let me make sure we're all friends first, that's all,' said the Australian, and added, 'You all kippers?'

'Kippers?' said Manning wearily, suspecting some sort of tasteless joke about cooking.

'Kippers. Don't you know? Two faces and no guts. Pommies. Brits.'

'Oh,' said Manning, 'some of us, yes.'

'I tell you frankly,' the young man continued, smiling graciously at his attendants as he spoke, 'this is not quite the scene I expected. Far from it. Been struggling through the bleeding jungle for nearly four weeks, heard in a bar in Moresby these little black bastards had gold and stuff up here, know anything about it, by any chance?'

His conversational pace was becoming too much even for Manning. 'You're getting on so well, you might suggest . . .'

'Don't rush me. These little tykes seem to have got it into their curly little heads that I'm, excuse the expression, Jesus Christ' ('Alleluia,' intoned the many pygmies who had remained on their knees since his arrival), 'Jesus Christ or something, way they're carrying on.'

'So Jesus Christ, gemme outa here,' spluttered Murgatreud.

'You would seem unusually well placed to attempt a miracle,' suggested Manning.

The Australian was game. 'Any along you speak along pidgin?' he addressed the crowd.

And, surprisingly perhaps, Goliath, a man little noted for his knowledge of languages or of scripture, stepped forward and strode up to the pot. From the full height of his five feet three inches he addressed his question specifically to O'Halloran.

'Big fella he Big Fella Number One Mista?'

O'Halloran was about to reply without hesitation, when Manning cut in. 'Puts you in a ticklish position, I fully

140

appreciate, but I should have thought it might be an occasion when a small white lie was in order.'

O'Halloran looked appalled at his dilemma.

'Gemme outa here,' repeated Murgatreud from across the water.

The most that O'Halloran could bring himself to do was to nod. But nod he did.

Goliath was delighted.

'Sure is a swell scheme,' chipped in the parrot, for the first time today.

'Sure is,' said Goliath, and he clapped his hands above his head, turning to the door of the compound. A few moments later a party of pygmies appeared on the other side of the door with a large and firmly constructed bamboo cross. The upright pole was about ten feet long, the cross bar at least six feet wide, and they were bound together with vines. Holes had been cut towards the two ends of the cross bar, precisely as in the miracle plays at York, and in them were loosely stuck what appeared to be the lethal points of two of Murgatreud's very latest spears.

'What's this, then?' asked the Australian, laughing nervously at the attendants who were still gently bathing his brow. Then he noticed that one of them held a vicious-looking ring of jungle thorns and briars, and before he had time to move it was forced down over his head and deep on to his forehead.

'EEeeeaaaaoooowwww, don't do that,' he yelled, for the pain was excruciating. Some pygmies were grabbing his hands, so he threw them off, and then he threw off some others who took their place, and yet some more, but it was a case of Gulliver against the Lilliputians, and eventually his hands were tied and the crown was firmly in place.

'Stop it, stop it, for God's sake stop it,' O'Halloran was now yelling from the pot. 'Oh, Mother of Mercy, what have we taught them, J.K., stop them, you could stop them, you know I was wrong to nod, this is not the Messiah, this not the Messiah, what have we taught them that they should under-stand so wrong, O Lord, what sins have we committed in our

teaching, stop, my children, stop, this is not the Second
Coming, the Second Coming will be entirely different from
this, entirely different . . .'

But no one listened, and the Australian had now been
whipped and driven and jeered through the door out of the
smithy compound into the open space in front of the white
men's huts. Here the cross was hoisted on to his back.
To hold such a large man, and yet leave him free to walk,
they attached a great many long vines round his waist. A
broad circle of pygmies held the other ends, all pulling
outwards. He was as secure as an ocean liner manipulated by a
dozen little tugs, or a wild horse controlled on long ropes by
those breaking him in. And so he passed out of sight, the
centre of a happy crowd which now began to sing, in strong
unison, but with considerable phonetic variations:

> 'There is a green hill far away,
> Without a city wall,
> Where the dear Lord was crucified,
> Who died to save us all.'

How often in scripture lessons had O'Halloran explained
this verse, describing the very position of Calvary outside the
walls of Jerusalem! And how precisely did the pleasant green
knoll, beyond the wall of the fort, between church and
hospital, fit his description.

XXXIX

The entire crowd had left, to witness the
greater of the two attractions. Only J.K. and Teresa remained

behind. Even J.K., showing traces of embarrassment, had attempted to slip away.

'Don't go,' said Manning.

The pygmy stayed, but like an awkward teenager now. He regretted that Manning and O'Halloran should share Murgatreud's fate, but had long ago decided not to admit as much to Goliath. He gazed now at the base of the pot, or at Teresa.

The girl knelt in her novice's robes, very upright, leaning slightly forward, with her palms pressed together in front of her bowed head. She was like a donor to one side of a painting of a martyrdom. Her eyes were closed, intensely closed. Her lips moved repetitively.

O'Halloran, too, was feverishly mumbling. His euphoria had been rudely shattered by the recent events. He now had a very great deal of hard praying to get through in the brief space of time before he expected to meet his Maker. He had closed his eyes for the better concentration, and Manning hardly expected to see them open again.

Murgatreud's head had flopped back against the side of the pot. The mouth was open, fractionally above the surface of the water, and the breath passed through it in a series of short gasps, no sooner in than out again.

Manning wondered whether he could find in himself the energy to tackle J.K. He felt strangely weary, even resigned to this supremely ludicrous end, the classic *reductio ad absurdum* of all their endeavours. He found that imminent death held no terrors, but the process of dying might well prove a different matter. It was several minutes since he had noticed, with wry interest, the approach and then the passing of $95 \cdot 1°$, the temperature which relieved the pain in his piles. Now tiny bubbles were rising to the surface of the water and skidding sideways before they popped. The heat on the knee-caps was intense.

'J.K.,' he called.

For the first time since the crowd had left, J.K. looked directly at his master.

'Yes? What?' He was hoping that the so-called stiff upper lip would get them both through this confrontation (he had been taught to ridicule the phrase but revere the concept). If Manning chose to conceal his pain behind a façade of detachment and irony, J.K. would be safe. A breakdown, a direct emotional appeal, would be entirely out of character and far more disturbing.

'I don't see what you can hope to get out of this,' said the teacher.

'You mean me? Personally?'

'Any of you.'

'Everything. Our own way. That's all.' J.K. deliberately focused his mind on images of celebration, firelit dance, spectacular parade, assembly, impassioned debate, and of himself discreetly behind the mighty Goliath (only by a pace or two, only for a year or two). These thoughts had sustained him in the past few dangerous days. They might serve to distract him now, while the temperature rose the next few crucial degrees.

'I mean our death,' continued Manning. 'Cause you trouble in the long run. Get rid of us, yes, of course. Let Murgatreud call the helicopter. Be gone by tomorrow. All three of us, and the Australian – even he's not beyond help if you hurry. Come on, J.K., admit it. You know I'm right. But you've got to be quick, it's getting damned hot in here. Feel it. Try your hand.'

J.K. declined to come so near. 'It's beginning to steam,' he said. 'Anyway, how could I stop them? Christ turning up for the Second Coming just as soon as they'd put you in the pot, kind of puts the lid on it.'

Manning winced. 'No need to be flippant.'

'I'm not. That must be the way they see it. Mustn't it?'

Murgatreud had been showing renewed signs of life, and at this moment, to J.K.'s relief, he suddenly interrupted.

'J.K.,' he spluttered. Water trickled into the corners of his mouth. He puffed it out in a feeble spray. 'Close, na?'

J.K., who had kept his distance from Manning, walked calmly now to the side of the pot. Murgatreud's eyes were open. He was gathering his strength, desperately, in one last bid for survival.

'Gooboy,' he gasped, and with a faint movement of the head through the water and a grotesque hint of a wink, he beckoned the pygmy even closer, black cheek by white jowl, for greater intimacy.

'Hey, amigo, lemme out, na? Outa pot?' The voice was a steamy whisper, wheedling. 'Like fa charity sake, howbowdat, huh? Fa liddel childern, na? Liddel childern no legs. Liddel childern no arms, J.K. Need Murgy, na? Tellya what. Outa pot today. Send Contact secret number fa liddel childern. Back in pot tomorra. Howbowdat? Fair deal, na? Jesfada childern, na?'

'Why not give *me* the number?' said J.K. 'We could use some Swiss francs, sooner or later. Why not, then? Why not give me the number?'

'So dooadeal, na?' gasped Murgatreud, who now looked like a pink football floating on the surface of the water.

'Just give me the number.'

'Wassa deal?'

'What's the number?'

'Deal,' groaned the face, in a deep long-drawn-out sigh. 'Na?'

There was silence. J.K. put his mouth close to the fat man's ear.

'Frankly, Murgatreud, you're a bit of a shit ...'

'Really, J.K.,' put in Manning. Certain responses were even now automatic.

'Yes, really,' continued the pygmy, 'he's a bit of a shit, no one would deny that. But we're probably better off now than we would have been without him.'

'That's generous.'

'*De mortuis nil nisi bonum*, what?'

Manning took the bait. '*Morituris*, please. For a few moments more. Very few more, by the feel of it.'

For the first time J.K. relaxed. He twirled the long straight bone through his nose.

'Granted,' he said, with a broad smile. 'Let's all enjoy one final moment of classical precision.'

The three faces were becoming blurred, floating in the

steam, disembodied, like theatrical effects. The priest's lips no longer moved, but Murgatreud suddenly spluttered again. Manning grimaced as he forced out some final words, above the pounding of his heart.

'Give him the number,' he said, towards Murgatreud's face, two feet away. And with a profound effort of will – for J.K., only for J.K. – he followed the simple advice with a reason. A reason might be enough to tip the balance, as he had plenty of time to tell himself, again and again, steeling his nerves, while he urged out the words, slow seething letter by letter, or so it seemed. 'It's their stuff.'

The gaunt head fell forward with a splash. J.K. moved as if to raise it then changed his mind. He turned instead to the puce balloon of Murgatreud's face, blank to the sky.

'You heard what the gentleman said,' he suggested, straight into what appeared to be the ear, 'give us the number.'

But it seemed that the flesh, as it had threatened for years, had at last swollen so far as to seal up for ever, under the pressure of its own conflicting masses, the last of the great entrepreneur's orifices. Certainly he heard not a word, and his eyes were closed – not with his lids but with the relentless puffing of cheek towards eyebrow, of eyebrow down to cheek.

So the precious secret was smothered too. Not a penny would reach the little children. As usual, only the Swiss would gain.

On the following pages are other recent paperbacks
published by Quartet Books.
If you would like a complete catalogue of
Quartet's publications please
write to us at 27 Goodge Street, London W1P 1FD

THE LUCK OF GINGER COFFEY
Brian Moore

The Luck Of Ginger Coffey is a brilliant example of Brian Moore's shrewd observation. Ginger Coffey is a thoroughly likeable failure; his new life in a new land (from Ireland to Canada) is hardly off the ground before it starts to crumble around him. At his lowest ebb, Ginger suddenly decides to fight back against his fate, and armed only with the luck of the Irish and a lot of bravado, he starts running uphill in hope, into a hilarious series of misadventures, disasters – and victories. *The Luck of Ginger Coffey* is a superbly entertaining novel.

Fiction 35p

THE PERFECT STRANGER
P. F. Kavanagh

This celebrated autobiography, winner of the Richard Hillary Memorial Prize for 1966, is as readable and funny as it is hauntingly tender. It is P. J. Kavanagh's tribute to the memory of his first wife, Sally, the perfect stranger – and it is also the absorbing, amusing tale of his early years, from schooldays and undergraduate life to the time he spent in Korea as a soldier and his happy, but short-lived, marriage to Sally.

'A real book; human, tender, gentle, loving, intelligent' – *Sheffield Morning Telegraph*

'A love story beautifully told' – *Sunday Telegraph*

Autobiography 40p

PEBBLES FROM MY SKULL
Stuart Hood

Pebbles from my Skull is a fascinating reflection on a way of life now almost vanished, and a vivid account of the dangerous life of a Resistance fighter.

'Combines the mesmeric readability of good modern fiction with a feeling of lived experience to which few novels can attain' – *Listener*

Autobiography 35p

ALL BULL: THE NATIONAL SERVICEMAN

Edited with an introduction by B. S. Johnson, with contributions from John Arden, Alan Burns, Mel Calman, Ian Carr, Edward Lucie-Smith, Michael Holroyd, Jeff Nuttall, Karl Miller, Alan Sillitoe and others.

It is now ten years since the last serviceman was 'demobbed'. *All Bull* recounts the experiences – funny, brutal, frightening, sometimes downright farcical – of twenty-four reluctant heroes, men from all walks of life who were obliged to undergo National Service.

Autobiography 50p

VANITY OF DULUOZ
Jack Kerouac

'A dazzling sunburst of white-hot prose' – *Tribune*

The Duluoz saga is known to thousands through such classics as *Desolation Angels* and *On The Road*: *Vanity Of Duluoz* relates the beginnings of the whole story from the day Jack Duluoz/Kerouac won an athletic scholarship to university up to his wild time in New York City just as the underground scene there was starting to simmer. In it Kerouac rushes headlong into a frontal assault on life, 'a total abandonment to feeling' (*Guardian*), producing a book that is every bit as brilliant as his modern classic *On The Road*.

Fiction 40p

PROTEST
J. P. Donleavy, Allen Ginsberg, Norman Mailer, Colin Wilson, Jack Kerouac, Kingsley Amis, John Wain and others

One of the most significant developments in post-war literature, on both sides of the Atlantic, was the meteoric rise of the realistic school of writing as practised by the authors in this book. Stripping away all pretention and hypocrisy, they wrote of truth, celebrating man as he is, and in the process brought to bear a powerful social criticism. They were the true spokesmen for their age. This is an important source book for all students of modern literature.
Edited by Gene Feldman and Max Gartenberg

Fiction 60p

AN ORKNEY TAPESTRY
George Mackay Brown
with drawings by Sylvia Wishart

George Mackay Brown is one of Scotland's most gifted poets and short story writers, whose work is universally acclaimed. He lives in Stromness, where he has always lived. *An Orkney Tapestry* is his testimonial to his native land, a celebration of the roots of a community which mixes history, legend, drama and folklore into a rich and varied tapestry.

'George Mackay Brown is a portent. No one else writes like this or has this feeling for language . . . His is an innate talent: as true as that of Yeats' – Jo Grimond, *Spectator*

Literature/Travel 50p

These books are obtainable from booksellers and newsagents or can be ordered direct from the publishers. Send a cheque or postal order for the purchase price plus 6p postage and packing to Quartet Books Limited, P.O. Box 11, Falmouth, Cornwall TR10 9EN